Will leaned across the seat and peered out Dena's window.

His bare thigh touched hers. The air was hot and his skin warm, yet she shivered. The hair on his leg tickled pleasantly, but she didn't feel like laughing. She wanted to lean against him, to rest her head on his chest.

She stole a glance at him. His attention was glued on her, not the terrain. His eyes were that warm chocolate color. There were gold flecks in his irises, like tiny droplets of sun.

His lids lowered as he stared at her mouth. Then he raised his gaze and searched her eyes.

Feigning thirst, she jerked her attention away and reached for bottled water. How could she get through the next three hours without making a complete fool of herself?

By keeping her head. She wasn't interested in Will, not the least bit.

Right. And the moon is made of Camembert cheese.

Dear Reader,

Around this time of year, everyone reflects on what it is that they're thankful for. For reader favorite Susan Mallery, the friendships she's made since becoming a writer have made a difference in her life. Bestselling author Sherryl Woods is thankful for the letters from readers—"It means so much to know that a particular story has touched someone's soul." And popular author Janis Reams Hudson is thankful "for the readers who spend their hard-earned money to buy my books."

I'm thankful to have such a talented group of writers in the Silhouette Special Edition line, and the authors appearing this month are no exception! In *Wrangling the Redhead* by Sherryl Woods, find out if the heroine's celebrity status gets in the way of true love…. Also don't miss *The Sheik and the Runaway Princess* by Susan Mallery, in which the Prince of Thieves kidnaps a princess…and simultaneously steals her heart!

When the heroine claims her late sister's child, she finds the child's guardian—and possibly the perfect man—in *Baby Be Mine* by Victoria Pade. And when a handsome horse breeder turns out to be a spy enlisted to expose the next heiress to the Haskell fortune, will he find an impostor or the real McCoy in *The Missing Heir* by Jane Toombs? In Ann Roth's *Father of the Year,* should this single dad keep his new nanny…or make her his wife? And the sparks fly when a man discovers his secret baby daughter left on his doorstep…which leads to a marriage of convenience in Janis Reams Hudson's *Daughter on His Doorstep.*

I hope you enjoy all these wonderful novels by some of the most talented authors in the genre. Best wishes to you and your family for a very happy and healthy Thanksgiving!

Best,

Karen Taylor Richman
Senior Editor

Please address questions and book requests to:
Silhouette Reader Service
U.S.: 3010 Walden Ave., P.O. Box 1325, Buffalo, NY 14269
Canadian: P.O. Box 609, Fort Erie, Ont. L2A 5X3

Father of the Year

ANN ROTH

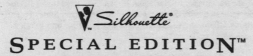

SPECIAL EDITION™

Published by Silhouette Books

America's Publisher of Contemporary Romance

In loving memory of Susan Holmberg.

I miss you, babe.

 SILHOUETTE BOOKS

ISBN 0-373-24433-9

FATHER OF THE YEAR

Copyright © 2001 by Ann Schuessler

This edition published by arrangement with Harlequin Books S.A.

® and TM are trademarks of Harlequin Books S.A., used under license. Trademarks indicated with ® are registered in the United States Patent and Trademark Office, the Canadian Trade Marks Office and in other countries.

Visit Silhouette at www.eHarlequin.com

Printed in U.S.A.

Books by Ann Roth

Silhouette Special Edition

Stranger in a Small Town #1356
Father of the Year #1433

ANN ROTH

has always been a voracious reader, reading everything from classics to mysteries to romance. Of all the books she's read, love stories have affected her the most and stayed with her the longest. "Is there anything more powerful and moving than a love that triumphs over seemingly insurmountable odds and ends in happily ever after?"

While in college she was lucky enough to meet and marry her own real-life hero. Today they live in the Seattle area with a finicky cat who rules the house. They have three wonderful college-age daughters.

It had long been Ann's dream to pen emotional love stories. In 1999 she won the Romance Writers of America Golden Heart Award for Best Long Contemporary with *Stranger in a Small Town*. Winning the prestigious award pushed her toward her goal: publication. "Yes, dreams can come true!" she says.

Ann would love to hear from readers. You can write her c/o P.O. Box 25003, Seattle, WA 98125-1903.

An essay by Harry Stoner,
8 years old

My dad should be Father of the Year. He let me live with him when Mom died. He'd never been a dad, and he didn't know me. I didn't think he liked me at first. He worked a lot and wouldn't go horseback riding. But then Dena came. Everyone called her my nanny, but she was my friend. She made Dad go horseback riding. It was fun! Dena and Dad are friends now too. Sometimes they even look at each other funny. That means they like each other. Gross. But if they got married, then I wouldn't only have the best dad, I'd have a whole new family!

Prologue

Will Stoner frowned into his speakerphone. "There must be some mistake. I've never fathered a child, not with Marie Landry or anyone else." He squeezed the bridge of his nose in a futile effort to forestall a pounding headache. "She must be after my money. That kid's not mine. He can't be."

"DNA tests don't lie, buddy. You *are* the father." Cal Rhinquist's blunt statement didn't surprise Will. His friend and chief counsel always cut straight to the point.

Will swore. Unable to sit, he stood and paced the perimeter of his spacious office, his footsteps muffled by plush cream carpet. From his thirtieth-floor window, he watched a brave sailboat lurch dangerously as it tried to navigate the choppy, winter waters of Puget Sound.

His stomach felt like that boat. "You know me, Cal. I'm always careful." Even during his brief, hellish marriage. "And I sure don't want kids." Not with his track record. "How could this have happened?"

Cal laughed humorlessly. "I wasn't there, but I assume the usual way. You and the mother got naked and..."

Will hadn't even thought of Marie Landry for years, until this whole mess had slapped him in the face a few weeks ago. He rubbed his neck and tried to remember back that far, finally letting out a heavy breath. "Yeah, but just once. The night I graduated from college."

Nine years ago, but it seemed like a lifetime. He'd been twenty-four then, and the only things he'd owned were an aging Carmen Ghia, a brand-new business degree and the fierce desire to succeed. There were no women in his life. With working, studying and keeping an eye on his kid brother, Mark, he hadn't had the time.

Vaguely he remembered Cal and Mark treating him to a few too many celebratory beers at a local tavern. After a couple of hours, both took off. But Will hadn't wanted to go home to his lonely studio apartment.

So he'd stayed at the bar and flirted with Marie, the long-legged, sandy-haired waitress who'd served him beer from time to time during his four years of college. She'd flirted back, and when her shift ended, had invited him home with her. Two days later he'd started a new job. By the time he thought to look her up again a few months down the road, she'd moved, leaving no forwarding address.

This was the woman who'd borne a son she

claimed was his. A full-fledged headache hammered his head. He groaned. "Maybe I drank too much, but I know I used protection. We had a good time, nothing more, and we never saw each other again."

"Well, that 'good time' turned into an eight-year-old son named Harry."

A son. *His* son. Strange feelings Will didn't understand rumbled through him. Surprise. Shock. And an unfamiliar warmth. He dropped onto his chair, the whisper of the soft, buttery leather oddly comforting. "I don't get it," he said, wondering aloud what he'd been pondering for weeks. "If Marie knew I was the boy's father, why didn't she tell me? Why wait until now, after a serious car accident?"

"Maybe she thought you'd try to take the kid away from her. But we'll never know for sure." Cal paused and cleared his throat. "She died over the weekend. There are no other living relatives."

Will swore softly, his anger displaced by grief and profound regret. For what might have been. For what *was*. Poor Marie. Poor Harry. "I'm sorry," he murmured.

He knew what it felt like for a kid to lose a parent. It hurt damned bad. At least he'd had a mother and little brother to share the pain. Harry, it seemed, had no one.

Except for Will. Dear God, he had a son.

What should he do now?

He glanced at the gold-framed motto hanging between two diplomas and a photocopy of his first one-million-dollar check. Do the Right Thing, it proclaimed. The words had always guided him down the best path. He knew what he had to do, what was right.

He straightened in his chair. "I want the boy to live with me."

"Good." Cal's tone carried his approval. "With four bedrooms and five baths, you've certainly got the room."

Will's secretary buzzed to remind him of a meeting. He swiveled his chair around to look out once again at the weather-whipped Sound. The sailboat had disappeared, perhaps seeking refuge until the wind quieted.

"I've got to run, Cal." Will turned back to the phone and switched into the problem-solving mode that had made his commercial real estate business a success. "Set things in motion, will you? The boy's in Sacramento. Bring him to Emerald Valley."

"That's been taken care of, at his end. He's flying up this afternoon, right after the funeral."

"Today?" Will rubbed a hand over his face. "I've got meetings until late tonight, and I fly to Denver first thing tomorrow. Can't you push things back a week?"

"Not possible. Harry's been staying with a family friend for the past few weeks. She can't keep him any longer."

How did that make the kid feel? Will wondered. No doubt lonely and unwanted. The thought evoked a pained grimace. "All right, I'll ask Mrs. Lettie to help." He pictured his twice-a-week housekeeper rubbing her hands at the prospect of cooking for the boy. "She can pick him up, bring him to the house and show him around. After that, he's on his own until the weekend."

"He's only eight, Will, not old enough to be on his own."

Will should have known that. He'd been the same age when his father had died. Before the funeral flowers had wilted, his mother had dubbed him "man of the house." How well he remembered the feeling of fear, of awesome responsibility. The role had robbed him of his childhood.

No young boy should have to grow up so quickly. Especially his own son. He flipped open his day planner and scanned it. "I'll see if I can shuffle those meetings, maybe lead a couple of conference calls instead."

"Since you run this corporation, that should be easy. Your problem is solved."

"There's more to my problems than moving a few meetings around." Will scribbled notes on a lined pad as he spoke. "For starters, I've got to get someone to look after the kid and enroll him in school."

He hung up, then buzzed his secretary. She bustled in, glasses in hand and pen and paper at the ready. "What do you need, Will?"

"Something's come up." He handed her a list of names and told her what to do. Then, leaning back in his chair, he steepled his fingers under his chin. "Please phone Mrs. Lettie and ask her to make up a spare bed and stock the refrigerator."

The middle-aged secretary nodded approvingly. "It's about time you had guests in to enjoy that gorgeous home of yours. You spend far too many hours away from it with your nose buried in work."

The mild scolding didn't surprise Will. His secretary rarely kept her opinions to herself. Something in his expression must have surprised her, because her brows lifted in curiosity. "Ah, so that's the way it is. Is she anyone I know? Maybe that model from Los Angeles?"

Will's mouth quirked. "Mind your own business."

"I will, now that you've taken my advice. It's good to see you dating again." She grinned. "Anything else? Dinner reservations? Tickets to a show?"

"There is one more thing." Will glanced at his notes, more to avoid her keen gaze than to remind himself what he'd written. "Get me the number of a reputable nanny agency. ASAP."

"You're dating a woman with kids." The secretary's eyes widened. "Will wonders never cease."

"This is no joke." Will fixed her with a level look. "You may as well know. I just learned that I have an eight-year-old son. Harry." He tested the name slowly, weighing it on his tongue.

"Oh, my heavens." The secretary's jaw dropped as she sank against the wall. "What does his mother...is she..." Her words sputtered to a halt.

"She's dead." Will swallowed. "I'm the boy's sole living relative."

"Poor little guy." His employee's eyes filled with sympathy. "What are you going to do?"

"Find a good school and a competent nanny." Will shook his head. "After that, I don't know."

Chapter One

One Month Later

Clutching her ticket and a battered carry-on, Dena Foster waited at the airline gate amidst a sea of milling passengers. One of them could well be her new employer, though, so far she hadn't spotted any men with young sons. Too bad she had no idea what Mr. Stoner looked like.

She bit her lip, wishing she'd asked Maggie, the owner of Nannies R Us, for a description. But when Maggie had offered her the job a few days ago, Dena had been too pleased and relieved to ask.

With her bank account down to ninety-two dollars, her roommate moving out to get married, and the lease about to expire on the tiny house they'd shared, the two-week job couldn't have come at a more opportune time—even if it was a bit out of the ordinary. She'd never nannied at a dude ranch.

She glanced down at her jeans and oversize pullover sweater. Was it suitable attire? She hoped sneakers were okay, because she didn't own boots and couldn't afford to buy a pair. She knew nothing about wanna-be cowboys struggling to lasso reluctant cattle through clouds of dust, which she imagined guests at the Wickenburg, Arizona, dude ranch did. She only knew that Mr. Stoner had planned a working vacation during his eight-year-old son Harry's spring break, and he needed Dena to oversee the boy.

She would have preferred a less rustic assignment. But she needed the work. Besides, if Mr. Stoner liked her and she and Harry got along, the job had potential to continue past the two weeks. And with the generous salary Mr. Stoner offered, she hoped it would.

Best of all, it sounded interesting, a way to use what she'd learned in her child psychology courses. A suddenly motherless boy now living with his estranged father in Emerald Valley, Washington, might need her help. Would definitely need it, from what Maggie had said. Apparently, it had been a difficult adjustment for both the boy and his father.

A nasal voice announced boarding, and passengers lined up at the gate. Dena glanced at her watch and for what felt like the hundredth time, scanned the area anxiously. Where were they?

The second boarding announcement came all too soon. Her stomach tightened in a flutter of nerves. Surely they'd show up. But what if they didn't? Over the weekend she'd packed all her things and moved them into storage, spending a chunk of her dwindling supply of cash in the process. If this job fell through, she had no place to go.

Suddenly two males entered the waiting area, a tall man and small boy. They must be the Stoners. At last. Dena released a relieved breath and, pasting a friendly smile on her face, hurried toward them. "Mr. Stoner?" She offered her hand. "I'm Dena Foster, from Nannies R Us."

He towered above her, his dark eyes appraising as they flickered over her. Dena felt as though he'd noted everything about her in an instant, from her baggy green sweater to her beige jeans to her old, but clean, sneakers.

Thankfully, he didn't look at her the way some men did, as if he wanted to swallow her whole. She worked hard at playing down her looks, at making herself presentable but not attractive. Since she was such a poor judge of men, she wanted them to leave her alone.

"Will Stoner."

His hand engulfed hers in a firm, impersonal grip. Unwelcome warmth jumped through her. She quickly pulled her fingers from his. With his broad forehead, straight nose, and wavy black hair, he was very good-looking, the kind of man women swooned over.

Not her, of course. She was here to do a great job and get an extended contract at high pay. Nothing more.

Something about him, his stance, or maybe the confident slant of his chin, reminded her of her Reese. Will was bigger than her ex-husband, yet held himself in the same self-assured way all powerful men seemed to share, with his shoulders squared and his head high, as if he owned the world.

As if he got what he wanted, when he wanted it. No matter who got hurt. Just like Reese. Nothing attractive in that.

Forcing the unpleasant thoughts aside, she focused on the child lagging behind. Unlike his large, dark father, the boy was scrawny and fair-skinned and blond. Freckles spattered across his nose and cheeks, and an endearing cowlick caused a tuft of hair to stick up from his crown. But his huge brown eyes looked exactly like his father's. As Dena moved toward the child, they fixed intently on her.

"Hello, there." She smiled. "You must be Harry."

The boy glanced hesitantly at his father before replying with a scowl, "Yeah, that's me."

"Pleased to meet you." Ignoring the hostile glare, she held out her hand. His eyes wide with surprise, he stared as if he didn't know what to do.

"Shake her hand, Harry," Will ordered.

Dena winced at his rough tone. He sounded like a sergeant, commanding a new enlistee.

The boy's face flushed. "Yes*sir*." He grudgingly complied, barely touching Dena's hand before dropping his arm.

Out of the corner of her eye, she saw Will stiffen, clearly miffed.

The strain between them was almost a palpable thing.

So that's how it was. Perhaps this was the reason that although Mr. Stoner paid top dollar, he had trouble keeping nannies in his employ. Dena knew she was their fourth nanny in as many weeks. She was determined to do a good job, to make this trip a success and gain long-term employment. Anxious to smooth things over, she again tried to draw Harry out. "Are you excited about this vacation?"

One narrow shoulder shrugged.

Will glanced at her, his expression apologetic. "Sure you are, son. We're both really looking forward to this," he replied without much enthusiasm. He didn't look any more pleased at the prospect of spending two weeks at the dude ranch than Harry did.

"Last call for the flight to Phoenix," the airline attendant announced.

"We'd better board." Will gestured Dena and his son forward.

They walked down the gateway in silence. Maggie had said things with the Stoners were "a little difficult." From what Dena observed so far, that was a gross understatement. The air between father and son was so thinly stretched, it made her stomach clench. No wonder they couldn't keep a nanny.

And she was going to be right in the middle of it for the next two weeks. She swallowed.

What had she gotten herself into?

What had he gotten himself into? Will wondered as he drove down the two-lane highway toward Wickenburg. The trip had barely started, and already he and Harry were at each other's throats. Much as it had been when Will and Mark were kids. The way it still was between them. Will rolled his shoulders to alleviate the tension. What was it about family that brought out the worst in him?

Luckily he'd rented an SUV for the drive from

Phoenix to Wickenburg. Harry could spread out in the back seat. As soon as they'd pulled out of the airport, the boy had reached for his portable CD player and plunked on his headphones. Will didn't mind. When Harry listened to music, he couldn't talk. And that meant no sniping.

Will's thoughts turned to the silent woman beside him. When the kid had slipped on those headphones, she'd stopped trying to make conversation. Now she stared out her window at the rocky, sandy terrain rolling by.

Maggie at Nannies R Us had said good things about Dena, that she was warm, intelligent and nurturing, but she hadn't mentioned her looks. And Harry's new nanny was one hell of a looker. She appeared to be a good seven to eight years younger than Will, in her midtwenties. A blonde with a severe hairstyle that made her look stiff and prim. Despite that, she had a model's face, even without makeup. She was one of those women blessed with creamy skin and big, blue eyes. Will glanced at her lips. And a soft, full mouth that begged a man's attention.

His blood stirred, and he turned his focus to the winding road. He'd do well to remember she was Harry's nanny. Besides, when she looked at him, she didn't show so much as a flicker of interest. Which was as it should be. A woman as attractive as Dena probably had a boyfriend. Lucky man.

A gigantic branching cactus perched on a rocky hill caught Will's eye, powerful and majestic against the deep-blue sky, and he turned his thoughts to the desert terrain, so different from the green hills of Emerald Valley. He glanced again at Dena. She wore shapeless, baggy clothes, but he'd bet underneath she had a body to match that face, with curves in all the right places. His body tightened.

For God's sake. It had been months since he'd been with a woman. His ugly divorce three years ago had taken its toll on his libido. Besides, he'd been too busy rebuilding the fortune his ex-wife had taken and then growing it some more. Then Harry had arrived, and there wasn't the time to pursue women. Now Will was paying the price with an overactive imagination.

He forced his thoughts to more urgent matters. Like putting Harry's nanny at ease. With her posture stiff and her hands locked in her lap, she looked uptight and uncomfortable. The way he and Harry had acted the past four hours, Will couldn't blame her. He didn't know how to apologize, so he settled for making casual conversation.

"Ever been to a dude ranch?" he asked.

"No, have you?" She shifted slightly, turning to face him.

Her prim little bun had loosened, and fine, wispy strands of hair floated around her cheeks. Will stifled the urge to reach over and brush them back.

He shook his head. "My lawyer, Cal, and his wife brought their kids here last year. They had a great time. And since Harry likes horses…" He let the words trail off and glanced in the rearview mirror to see if his son had heard.

Despite the music, he had. Pulling off the earphones, he leaned forward. Faint strains of rock music filtered through. "We get to keep the same horse for two weeks, and we can groom and feed him, too. I'm going to ride all day long, every single day," Harry proclaimed, at last sounding like an excited eight-year-old.

Then he seemed to catch himself, as if he hadn't meant to open up. He promptly clamped his lips shut and settled the familiar scowl on his face.

Will frowned back. There were supposed to be plenty of kids at the ranch. Between them and the horses, maybe Harry would make friends.

Will wanted his son to fit in, if only for the two weeks they were here. The boy hadn't adjusted well to Emerald Valley. He hadn't made friends at the private school he was enrolled in, and his grades were poor. Will hoped a change of scenery would help. If things worked out, he might even buy his son a horse.

Right now though, he just wanted to see the kid crack a grin. Just once.

"Do you like horses, Dena?" the boy asked.

She turned around and smiled at him, a bright, dazzling smile that had Will sucking in a breath. "To tell you the truth, Harry, I don't know. I've never been near one."

"Neither has *he*." Harry pointed at Will. "But I have. My mom took me riding last year, when I was seven. She said I'm a natural."

"Is that so?" Dena looked impressed. "Maybe you can teach your dad and me."

The boy's scowl deepened as he glanced at Will. "*He*'s not going to ride, he's going to work."

Will grimaced. Harry called him, "you" and on occasion, "Will," but never "Dad." That stung. "Some of us have to earn a living," he said, his tone more stern than he intended. "That's how we can afford a five-star ranch like Golden Spurs."

Harry rolled his eyes and jerked on his earphones. With luck he'd leave them on, and they'd finish the drive in peace.

Dena's unhappy gaze darted from Will to the boy and again to Will. She looked as if she wanted to turn around and head back to Emerald Valley. "How long until we get there?"

"Half an hour, I'd guess."

She bit her lip. "After we check in, I'd like to talk to you in private," she said in a voice low enough that Harry couldn't hear.

"Sure," Will replied.

It didn't take a genius to know what she wanted to discuss. She was quitting already, before she even started. Just like the three previous nannies. His spirits sank like a stone in a pond. Dammit, not this time. Hadn't his kid suffered enough instability?

Besides all that, Will needed this woman. Stoner Enterprises was about to close a huge land deal up near the Canadian border, a great location for a new shopping center, and he needed to consult with Cal daily. And through Cal, he wanted to keep an eye on Mark, make sure his brother continued to show up at work every day. Then there were the potential business associates to meet with while he was here. He couldn't do all those things and watch Harry, too.

But that wasn't all, he acknowledged with brutal honesty. The truth was, he needed someone to act as a buffer between him and Harry. Without Dena, Will and his son would have to deal with each other directly. He had never been good at that. Look at what had happened with Mark. The idea of messing up

Harry the same way scared Will spitless. His grip on the steering wheel tightened.

"Is everything okay?" Dena asked, angling her head. A tiny pucker appeared between her brows.

"Never better," Will lied, working to keep the desperation out of his tone.

Her frown deepened, and she looked as if she wanted to ask another question. He forced a reassuring grin. "There's a turnoff somewhere around here," he said, to distract her. "Better keep an eye out for it."

While they both watched the road, he searched his mind for ways to persuade her to stay. Money always worked. He'd up her wages, offer her a credit card to buy whatever she wanted.

Anything to keep her here with him and his son. Because if she stayed, if she kept Harry occupied, maybe the boy wouldn't realize the horrible truth.

Will Stoner, rich and successful in the business world, was a miserable failure as a father.

Chapter Two

"There it is, on the right." *Finally.* Heaving a mental sigh of relief, Dena pointed to the large wooden Golden Spurs Ranch sign stuck in the sandy ground amidst the scrub and cacti. An hour and a half in the emotionally charged car had turned her into a keyed-up bundle of nerves.

Will turned into a long, paved road, cruising slowly past well-groomed buildings, a golf course populated with men and women and a double tennis court. A group of children, rackets in hand, clustered around a man in tennis whites for what was obviously a lesson. In the distance low mountains the color of deep amethyst filled the horizon against a flawless blue sky.

"Oh, my," Dena murmured. This wasn't the rustic ranch she'd imagined. "I can see why this place rates five stars."

"Like it?" Will glanced at her, his expression unreadable.

"So far."

He nodded, and some of the tension eased from his shoulders, though Dena didn't know why. His mouth quirked to a half grin, and the worry in his eyes faded.

Without that ever-present forbidding frown, he was even better looking. Sexy. Dena's pulse quickened. Flushing, she quickly turned away and stared out the window. "Look, Harry, there's the corral."

Both she and Will glanced in the rearview mirror. Earphones still firmly planted on his ears, the boy stared wide-eyed at the slatted wood fence and large red barn. But he didn't speak, and he didn't remove the earphones. He hadn't said a word since he'd slipped them back on after his brief, unhappy exchange with Will about working while they were here.

Will's hopeful expression faded. He opened his mouth, then clamped it shut. Dena frowned. She may not have her psychology degree yet, but anyone could see that Harry's actions stemmed from resentment. He'd suffered a huge loss when his mother died. He needed reassurance and plenty of attention. Didn't Will realize that?

A moment later he pulled into the parking lot and shut off the engine. "You and Harry wait here while I check in."

Dena nodded. Later she planned to share her insights with Will while they reviewed how he wanted her to handle his son. For now, unable to sit a moment longer, she opened her door. "Harry?" She waved to get his attention. "Want to stretch your legs?"

His face carefully blank, he tugged off the earphones. "What for?"

"To get a better look at the ranch." Determined to start off this vacation on the right foot, despite the huge chip on the boy's shoulder, she smiled. "Come on."

"I don't need to look," he grumbled, but he followed her.

They ambled around the car, to a concrete path a few feet away. Shading her eyes from the brilliant afternoon sun, Dena surveyed the area. "Look at those mountains." She gestured toward the horizon. "I've never seen so much open space. Isn't it beautiful here?"

Harry turned his gaze toward the mountains, then slowly scanned the white, clustered adobe guest cottages with their red-tiled roofs and sculpted desert yards. "It's different," he said. "Quiet."

"You're right." Dena had always lived in bustling cities—first Seattle and now the smaller but equally busy town of Emerald Valley. The stillness here touched something inside her, a need for silence she hadn't known she possessed. She breathed deeply. "What's that unusual smell? Why, it's clean air."

Harry didn't smile, but at least the furrows in his brow disappeared. "The horses weren't in the corral. I wonder where they are?" he asked, looking up at her.

"On their afternoon trail ride," Will replied in a gruff voice. He'd come up behind them so quietly they hadn't heard.

The boy's scowl returned, and he kicked a loose rock. "Oh."

Dena glanced at Will to see if he noticed, but he was busy opening the trunk. "Our cabin's not far from here. Let's take the bags over, Harry," he ordered in a tone that made her wince. "Then we'll look around."

The boy's eyes narrowed, full of hostility, but he obeyed. Dena didn't blame him for being angry. The way Will barked at his son in that stern voice upset her, too. She pressed her lips together. Someone needed to set the man straight. Human beings, and especially children, responded better to kindness and affection than gruffness.

But would he listen? She doubted it. She'd had firsthand experience with dictatorial men, during her disastrous marriage to Reese. Still, she had to try. She glanced at Harry, his narrow shoulders stooped under more than the weight of his bag. Thank goodness her ex-husband hadn't wanted children. If he had, where would she be now?

Hefting her and Harry's carry-ons, she followed Will and the boy down a winding sidewalk, past neatly kept cabins, each with a landscaped yard of raked sand, cacti and colorful low-lying, leafy plants she didn't recognize.

At last, Will set down the bags. "Here it is." He opened the door.

Harry entered first. Stopping in the tiled entry, he set down the bags and glanced around. "Wow," he breathed, his hostility momentarily forgotten.

Will's brows lifted, and his expression lightened a notch, as if he were relieved. "Go ahead," he said, gesturing Dena forward.

She stepped into a suite as luxurious as any she'd

shared with Reese. This one had a massive fireplace and a well-stocked wet bar in the spacious living room. One wall, made of glass, contained a sliding door leading onto a private patio complete with table, umbrella and lounging chairs. Beyond, the desert and mountains were clearly visible.

Will moved the bags inside. "There are three bedrooms. Choose the one you want, Harry."

"Okay," the boy replied tonelessly, but there was a distinct lift in his step as he headed down the hall.

When they were alone, Dena turned to Will. "This is lovely."

"Thanks." To her surprise, he flushed. "I just hope my son likes it here."

It was the opening she needed. She drew in a breath. "About Harry—"

"Not now." Leaning toward her, he lowered his voice. "We'll talk later, when he's asleep."

He was so close, she felt the heat from his body. He smelled like expensive cologne and man, a lethal combination that stirred unwelcome warmth inside her. She wanted to move away, but couldn't, not just yet. The look in his eyes, vulnerable and pleading, yet full of resolve, held and puzzled her.

Who was this man?

In an instant his expression heated and filled with awareness. *Sexual* awareness. To Dena's shock, her heart skittered wildly. She quickly retreated a step and dropped her gaze.

Clearing his throat, Will turned away. "I'll get the rest of the bags," he said, and slipped through the door.

It closed with a soft click. Dena wandered to the

coffee table, picked up a colorful booklet about the ranch and thumbed through it. There were pictures of smiling families riding horses, hiking, even soaring through the sky in hot-air balloons, but she barely noticed.

The unthinkable had happened. For the first time since her divorce three years earlier, she was attracted to a man. To Will Stoner, a powerful, wealthy, cold man, not unlike her ex-husband. Horrified, she dropped the booklet. What was the matter with her? Hadn't her failed marriage taught her anything?

This just proved again that she had absolutely no taste in men. Distraught, she hurried down the hall, searching for the bathroom. Closing the door behind her, she switched on the light and frowned at her flushed reflection. If she ever dated again, she'd choose a man who knew how to laugh and enjoy life. A man unafraid to show affection, who put people before business.

The exact opposite of Mr. Will Stoner. She'd do well to remember that. Besides, if she wanted this job to last, she must be professional and focused on Harry at all times. Not his father. Stern-faced, she took down her hair and refastened it into a nice, tight bun. Maybe she was just tired from a long day traveling. She splashed cool water on her cheeks. Yes, that was it. Will Stoner didn't attract her the littlest bit.

By the time he returned, she'd managed to convince herself of that. For the rest of the afternoon, while they toured the vast ranch, she maintained a safe distance, focusing on the boy at her side. Though the sights distracted and lulled him into a tentative truce with his father, his hostility and Will's stiffness lurked beneath the surface.

A huge cavern existed between them, and they definitely needed help to close it. Her help. She pressed her lips together. No matter that she was still two years short of earning her psychology degree. With two weeks at the ranch and a little assistance from her, the relationship between father and son was bound to improve.

She imagined a grateful Will, thanking her for her help and maybe inviting her to stay on at the end of the trip. And of all the money she'd earn, she could fill her savings account and put away enough to finish school. Yes, things were sure to work out for everyone.

Just as the sun set low on the horizon and a spectacular, pink-orange sunset washed the sky, a bell tolled in the distance. Will nodded as if he'd expected it. "That's the dinner bell. We'd better head back and dress."

"What did you say?" Dena asked. Maggie hadn't mentioned anything about this.

"We have to wear dumb-old jackets and ties," Harry grumbled. He eyed her Levi's and sweater. "You have to wear a dress."

"Oh?" She'd only brought two nice outfits. She pictured changing from jeans to the jumper or skirt set, over and over, and groaned. "For every meal?"

"It's not that bad." Will's mouth quirked. "The dress rules are only for dinner. The rest of the time jeans are fine."

With the harsh lines of his face softening and the sinking sun at his back, he looked more handsome than ever. Dena's stomach fluttered. From hunger, she decided. Because she positively, absolutely was not attracted to Will Stoner.

Period.

Why would a beautiful young woman like Dena wear that old, loose dress? Will wondered from his seat across the round, linen-covered dinner table. With her looks, she could have been the dining room's main attraction. Instead she'd played down her beauty in that uptight-librarian hairdo and a shapeless gray shift that had seen better days.

Even so, several men noticed her. Will watched one suck in his belly and another smooth back his artsy ponytail as they passed the table.

He frowned, for some reason irritated, and fought back the irrational urge to lift each man by his expensive lapels and toss him into the Olympic-size swimming pool just outside.

Dena was with him. As an employee, but those men didn't know that. He didn't want anything to interfere with her job. That was what bothered him, he decided. He glanced at her, but she didn't seem to notice either his disapproval or the men who caused it. Her attention was focused solely on the boy beside her.

"How's the fudge cake, Harry?" she asked in a tone that conveyed genuine fondness.

The boy swallowed and wiped his mouth before replying. "Good."

She looked as pleased as if she'd baked it herself, an expression Will wanted to see more of. When her generous mouth curled into a smile like that, she lit up the table.

"My flan is delicious," she said. "Would you like to taste it?"

For a moment the boy eyed her dessert with interest. Then his expression closed. "No, thank you." Bowing over his half-eaten dessert, he forked another mouthful.

Dena arched her brows and that attractive smile disappeared.

Frustration rolled through Will. The kid had yet to smile, though God knew, Dena had tried to coax a grin from him throughout the sumptuous meal. In vain. Harry wasn't about to lighten up, and they all knew it.

Dena seemed undaunted, asking soft-spoken questions and offering friendly comments designed to draw out the boy. Yet he spoke only when necessary, and then, mostly in one-syllable replies.

Will fought a growing sense of despair that was all too familiar. Bad enough he'd failed with his kid brother, Mark. Mark was doing okay now, but it had taken nearly thirty years for that to happen, no thanks to Will. He was older now and supposedly wiser. And damn, he didn't want to mess this up. Since Harry had moved in, Will had bought him new clothes, a computer, the latest video games, and a neon-blue bicycle with all the extras. None of it had brought the boy the pleasure Will had hoped for.

What would it take to make his son happy?

He glanced at Dena. The lovely new nanny couldn't hurt matters. She'd probably help. If she stayed.

The pucker between her brows worried him. He knew what it meant. Luxurious surroundings weren't enough. Like the other nannies, she couldn't handle the tension or Harry's sullenness. She planned to quit, head back to Emerald Valley.

Dread filled him. She couldn't leave—he wouldn't let her. For Harry's sake. The boy needed this vacation, and Will needed Dena to see it through.

He still didn't have a clear strategy for persuading her to stay, but he'd damn well do it. He was an excellent strategist. Didn't his net worth and success in the real estate business attest to that? If he could induce hard-headed businessmen to do his bidding, surely he could convince Harry's nanny to stay.

Just then a tall, bow-legged, jeans-clad cowboy wearing a black Stetson and a bola fastened with a huge silver eagle sauntered to the table. He stopped beside Harry, whose eyes were wide with wonder, and tipped his hat. "Evenin', folks. I'm Foreman Bob, and I manage the horse and riding programs here at Golden Spurs. Anybody in the family riding tomorrow?"

"I am," Harry replied with more enthusiasm than he'd shown all day. He sat up straight. "My name's Harry. I rode a horse once last year, and I'm a good rider."

"Great, Harry." Bob made a notation on his clipboard.

"Dena will go with you," Will added. If he signed her up for riding, she couldn't quit yet.

Her eyes widened, and he tensed, bracing for the excuse that foretold her resignation.

"But I don't know how to ride," she protested.

Maybe she didn't want to quit in front of Harry, or better yet, she'd decided to stay through tomorrow. Spared the worst for the moment, Will released a breath he hadn't known he held.

"No problem, ma'am," the cowboy reassured. "Around here, we take things slow and easy. We'll start you and the boy on a walking ride. That's where we teach you how to handle your horse. Once you get comfortable with that, we'll take more adventurous trips."

"Well..." Dena bit her lip and looked at Harry. "Do you mind if I come with you?"

He fiddled with his napkin. "I guess not."

A quick smile brightened her face. "Then please sign me up."

"Good decision." Bob's eyes flared with sudden interest, and Will knew her smile had captivated the man.

Damn cowboy better not step out of line... Will's hands tightened in his lap, and his eyes narrowed.

"What about you, sir?" Bob asked, his expression a mask of innocence.

Wondering at his sudden, irrational possessiveness, Will shook his head. What was the matter with him tonight? "Count me out," he growled. He'd work while Dena and Harry rode.

Harry slouched in his chair, and Dena's eyes widened. She pursed her mouth and shot Will a look that made him feel guilty, as though he'd done something wrong.

His mood blackened. Now what? They knew this was a working vacation.

Seemingly unaware of the tension ricocheting

around the table, Bob told them when to meet at the corral. With a friendly nod he headed for another table.

Several uncomfortable minutes ticked by, while Will and Dena finished their coffee and Harry stabbed listlessly at his half-eaten piece of cake. Neither she nor the boy spoke or looked at Will.

For some reason he felt like an ogre. He didn't like it. And he couldn't sit any longer. His cup clattered against the saucer. "Time to head back to the cabin." He stood. "I want to check in with Cal."

Casting him a look that promised a difficult conversation later, Dena set down her coffee and rose beside him. She touched the boy's head. "Come on, Harry. It's late, and you've got to get to bed."

"But I'm on vacation," he complained. "Can't I stay up?"

He looked to Will. For once, his eyes held a plea instead of resentment. Will was surprised and pleased. Glad to put off that talk with Dena a little longer, and at the same time, gain a few points with his son, he shrugged. "Fine with me."

Harry flaunted the small triumph by lifting his chin and smirking at Dena. A beat later, a yawn escaped from his mouth.

She shook her head. "I don't think staying up is a good idea, Harry, and I'm sure your father doesn't, either. You both heard what Foreman Bob said." She met Will's eye with a raised brow. When he gave a barely noticeable nod, she continued. "Our lesson starts early tomorrow morning. You don't want to be tired for that, do you?"

Will braced for an argument. To his amazement the boy gave in.

"I guess not," he muttered. Despite his tone, he seemed relieved.

Will felt anything but relief as they headed through the dining room and walked down the softly lit path toward the cabin. Harry needed a shower, and after that, a few minutes to settle into his temporary bedroom. With luck, that gave Will a scant hour more to plan his strategy.

Then it was time for that talk, time to persuade Dena to stay. He would make that happen—no matter what it took.

Will stood in front of the glass patio door and stared out into the night as he waited for Dena to come back from checking on Harry. The time for their talk had arrived.

He could close huge, complicated business deals. Getting her to stay should be a snap. Still, he needed a drink.

Pivoting, he strode to the well-stocked bar. He poured two fingers of brandy into a crystal snifter, swirled it gently and drank. The amber liquid tasted rich and smooth, and settled warmly in his stomach. He tasted again, then poured one for Dena.

Her footsteps echoed on the tile hallway and then whispered softly over the living room rug as she moved toward him. "Nightcap?" he asked, handing her the snifter. He glanced in the direction of Harry's room, just down the hall. "Is he asleep?"

"I think so." Dena swirled her glass, sniffed the

contents and sipped as if she drank expensive brandy often. "Thank you."

Her smile warmed him like the alcohol. "My pleasure."

He grinned back and let the heat he felt show in his eyes. Bad move. Her lips straightened, as did her spine. Jerking her gaze from his, she frowned at her drink. "Now that Harry's asleep, we should talk."

"Of course." He'd just crossed a line he hadn't meant to cross, sent out signals he had no business or intention of sending. His lack of control irritated him. For God's sake, she worked for him. Did he want to make matters worse, give her a legitimate reason to walk out?

A day away from the office and the clean, dry air made him feel lazy, not quite himself. That was why he reacted to her like a kid with an overabundance of hormones. He cleared his throat. "It's a nice night. We'll sit on the patio."

He flipped on the outside lights, slid open the glass doors and gestured her forward. Her scent, light and sweet, floated toward him through the balmy night air. Without meaning to, he sniffed appreciatively.

He waited until she chose a padded lawn chair, then took the one across from her. Tugging her skirt down past her knees, she crossed her legs demurely. What nice legs they were, long and slender. Will set his drink on the small redwood table beside him and stared out at the dark landscape beyond the patio.

Relying on a strategy that usually gained him the upper hand, he waited for Dena to start the conversation. Once she did, he'd bowl her over with his generosity, rolling over her objections before she knew what happened.

For a moment she said nothing, just sipped her brandy. Absolute quiet settled around them like a cocoon. She glanced up at the sky, exposing the long, pale column of her neck. "Look at the stars," she said, at last breaking the silence. "Even with the lights on, they're amazing. Like diamonds scattered across the heavens."

"Beautiful," he murmured, unable to take his eyes from her. He'd always liked a woman's neck, and hers was near perfect. He wanted to explore it with his lips, taste the sensitive place below her ear and make her shiver.

But this was no time for fantasies he didn't intend to pursue. Dragging his gaze from her, he picked up his drink. Dena was here to take care of his son, and he had no wish to complicate matters. He had a job to do. He had to convince her to stay. If she knew what he was thinking about right now, she'd quit for sure. "Ready for a refill?" he asked.

"No, thanks."

She squared her shoulders and sent him a no-nonsense look, and suddenly he felt like an amateur boxer about to step into the ring. *Here it comes,* he thought, and braced for her resignation.

"I need to know the ground rules."

"Ground rules," he repeated, puzzled.

"The way you want me to handle Harry." She leaned forward. "For example, do you want me to discipline him? If so, when should he—"

Will cut her off with a gesture. "Let me get this straight. You're not quitting."

Her brow creased as she angled her head. "Why would I do that?"

Thank God. Relief flooded him, and he sank gratefully against the seat cushion. "The last three women I hired quit, because of the way things are between Harry and me. As you no doubt noticed, his attitude isn't exactly warm and welcoming."

She shook her head. "Oh, no, Mr. Stoner, I'm not—"

"Will," he corrected.

"Will. As I was saying, I'm not the kind of person to back out because there are problems between you and your son, or because he's uncomfortable around me. He needs time to get used to me. That's only natural. I intend to do everything I can to earn his acceptance. And to be totally honest with you, I like the salary you pay and the potential for an extended contract." She paused to sip her drink. "So, how do you want me to handle discipline?"

Will liked her honesty. And he was so pleased she'd decided to stay, he didn't care how she handled Harry. He grinned. "From what I've seen, you're doing fine. I trust your judgment. Why don't we discuss the problems as they come up."

Dena shook her head. "That's not always possible. Look at what happened tonight. You said Harry could stay up, and I thought he should go to bed. It would be better for him and easier on us if we set rules in advance."

As a boy in the role of man of the house, Will had set his own rules while his mother worked two full-time jobs to keep them from starving. He'd learned the hard way that he needed a certain amount of sleep to function well, and the experience hadn't hurt him a bit. It probably wouldn't hurt Harry to learn the same way.

Then again, that same logic had backfired big-time with Mark. Will wanted none of that this time around. That thought and the earnest look on Dena's face convinced him she was right.

He shrugged. "If that's what you want, fine. From now on you set Harry's bedtime. If he does something you don't approve of, come to me, and we'll talk about it. Otherwise I'll expect him to obey you and do what you say. I'll tell him first thing tomorrow." He paused. "Satisfied?"

"It's a start." She pursed her lips in that scolding-schoolteacher way, and Will knew the discussion was far from finished.

Now what? A sense of dread settled in his belly. "But?" he prodded.

"Why aren't you riding with Harry and me tomorrow?"

"You think I should spend more time with him, is that it?" He waited for her nod, then shook his head. "Trust me, he doesn't want me along." Admitting the truth hurt, even though, deep down, the idea of spending time with his son scared him.

"That's not true. Harry *wants* to be with you. He just doesn't know how to say it."

To Will's chagrin, she fixed him with a look of concern. He frowned. He didn't want or need her pity, but he *did* want her to understand. "What did Maggie tell you about Harry and me?"

"That he used to live with his mother and that she recently died in a car accident." Dena's expression filled with sympathy. "I can't imagine how that feels. It's so sad."

"Yes, it is." Will's chest hurt for his son as he finished his drink. Brushing away his feelings, he fixed her with a level gaze. "Did Maggie tell you that before the accident, I didn't know Harry existed, and he had no idea who his father was?"

He saw by Dena's expression that he'd surprised her.

"What do you mean?" she asked. "I thought you were divorced."

"I am, but not from Marie—Harry's mother." Dena looked even more confused, so Will explained. "Nine years ago, his mother and I, uh, slept together. Just once. She left town without telling me she was pregnant. By the time Harry was old enough to understand, I was married. Without ever contacting me, Marie told him I didn't want him." Saying the words aloud didn't ease Will's pain or the anger that simmered in him each time he thought about what Marie had done. His hands clenched at his sides.

Dena's eyes widened. "Is it true?"

"That I didn't want him?" The question stung. "Hell, no. He's my son, my flesh and blood. How could I not want him? But he doesn't believe that." Will stared into the depths of his empty glass. "I just wish Marie had given me the chance to be a father from the beginning. Then things might have been different."

He might have married her instead of Becky and avoided a ton of pain and misery. But Marie hadn't told him. Her mistake had left behind a resentful boy who didn't want or trust Will. Who didn't believe he cared. Will didn't have a clue how to change that. His chest hurt again.

Dena bit her lip. "But that's so unfair."

"That's an understatement." Will's laugh was bitter. "Right now we're, uh, going through a rough period, still getting used to each other." He didn't add that, instead of improving, their relationship had steadily worsened. "I brought Harry here because he likes horses. I want him to have a good time. That's *my* ground rule."

"Then we agree on that."

Those damned lips pursed, and he knew she wasn't finished yet. He frowned. "Go on."

"If you're serious about making this fun, you and Harry should do things together. He needs to be with you, and you need to be with him. With so much to offer in the way of activities here, you've got the perfect opportunity."

Open up new ways for Harry to scorn and reject him? Masking the pain that thought engendered, Will shot her the narrow-eyed look he used to make opponents squirm. "The way I deal with my son is my business. Your job is to see to his needs and keep him busy."

She didn't even flinch, instead raised her head stubbornly. "I think you're making a mistake."

Most people backed down from him. Even though Dena infuriated him, he had to admire her courage. "What are you, a psychologist?"

"I will be, as soon as I graduate. My specialty is children, so I know what I'm talking about. Come riding with us."

To make a fool of himself on some horse? The kid

would have a field day with that. Will scoffed. "You don't give up, do you? I can't spare the time. There are important things happening at my company, and I've got several conference calls lined up." He blew out a breath. "How clear can I make it? I hired *you* to spend time with my son."

"And I will. You'll be glad I'm here, I promise." Her mouth did its pursing act again. "At least walk us to the corral in the morning."

The woman was tenacious as a pit bull. Will rolled his eyes. "All right. Now are you satisfied?" He glanced pointedly at his expensive watch.

"No." She smiled. "But tomorrow's another day."

Groaning inwardly, he stood, then offered her a hand up. Her fingers felt small and delicate inside his palm before she slid them away. But underneath she wasn't delicate at all. She was stubborn and determined to push him and Harry together, no matter how painful or difficult that might be. His lips thinned.

In the living room she turned to him. "Good night, Will, and sweet dreams."

This time, he was too annoyed to let that mouth affect him. He drew his brows together. "I don't dream." Not since he was Harry's age.

"Oh. Well, in case that changes, sweet dreams, anyway."

Will watched her leave the room. Her long, graceful stride stirred his blood. At the same time her meddling annoyed the hell out of him. He scrubbed his face with his hands and wished he'd never laid eyes on Dena Foster. If he didn't need her so badly... But he did. And she was staying without a raise or any added perks.

Bottom line, she hadn't quit on him.

He rubbed his chin thoughtfully. Irritating or not, maybe, just maybe, she'd stick around awhile.

She was attractive, too, though Will didn't intend to dwell on that. In fact, he planned to push all those intriguing sexual thoughts of her from his mind and focus instead on Dena and Harry and how they related. Who knew, by the end of this vacation, they could end up never wanting to see each other again. She wouldn't be the first nanny his son had sent packing.

Regardless, it was going to be an interesting two weeks.

Chapter Three

The alarm clock's loud *beep-beep-beep* cut into Dena's dreams much too soon. Was it already time to get up? Groaning, she groped for the snooze button, noting the gray, predawn light that crept in through the window. It was early yet. Fifteen more minutes couldn't hurt.

She snuggled back under the covers and closed her eyes. Unfortunately, thoughts and images flooded her mind, the same ones that had kept her up for hours last night.

All of them about Will Stoner. Now there was a complex man. The remote business side of him exuded a cool confidence that was unnerving and reminded her of her ex-husband, Reese. She wrinkled her nose in distaste.

But Will was also a father, and in that arena, he

was anything but competent. He hid his shortcomings under a gruff take-charge manner, but that didn't fool her. Inside, uncertainty and vulnerability ruled.

The poor man had been through plenty. To suddenly find out about an eight-year-old son was shock enough. But to learn what the boy's mother had done, keeping him from his father, telling him his father didn't want him, must hurt unbearably. Her heart squeezed in sympathy, and she hugged her spare pillow to her chest.

Last night Will had talked about his son in ways that left no doubt as to the depth of his feelings. But he didn't seem to know how to show Harry what he felt.

Stiff and nervous, he addressed the boy in stern, soldierly tones. And he made excuses to keep them apart. Dena clucked with disapproval.

With that kind of behavior, who could fault the eight-year-old for his adult-size resentment?

Not that Harry made it easy. He retreated behind a scornful facade, one that rivaled his father's. The two floundered around each other like fish on dry land.

A dire situation but not hopeless. Especially with her help. Though flat on her back, Dena squared her shoulders and renewed her pledge to bring them together. Harry needed a protector, someone who could gain his trust and speak out for him. And Will needed to relax and open up.

She knew how to help Harry, by showing him her trust and respect and by giving him the attention and affection he craved. With time and patience, she'd gain the same things from him.

But his father... Will preferred to give advice rather

than take it. Only he didn't advise, he ordered. Dena pressed her lips together. When her marriage had finally ended, she'd made up her mind never again to let a man bully her. That included her present employer.

She pictured Will, stern-faced and stiff-shouldered, and shook her head. Getting him to loosen up wasn't going to be easy.

Maybe if she relaxed first… Unbidden, she thought about last night, when he'd handed her a glass of brandy. His eyes, normally a cool, impersonal brown, had warmed to rich chocolate. That look could melt snow.

A long sigh escaped her lips. It had certainly scrambled her brain, enough that she'd momentarily forgotten that she wasn't attracted to him. Even now, as she remembered that heated look, her nerves hummed.

Dismayed, she bolted upright just as the snooze alarm beeped. She slapped it into silence, then threw back the covers. Will wasn't her type, he really wasn't. He was a workaholic, too much like Reese. Plus she worked for him. Maggie had strict rules about things like that. Besides, how could she help the man if every time he looked at her, her pulse raced and her thoughts clouded?

"There'll be no more of that," she sternly vowed as she slipped into the luxurious terry robe that hung in her closet, courtesy of Golden Spurs Ranch. Gathering her clothes, she padded toward the bathroom shared with Harry. She'd shower and dress, then wake him in time for the breakfast bell.

At this hour the cabin was still and quiet. Will had

promised to escort them to the corral later. Did he plan to join them for breakfast, too, or did he expect her and Harry to eat alone?

She hoped not. Some of her fondest childhood memories stemmed from breakfasts and dinners with her parents. No matter how busy they were, they came together as a family twice a day, every day, to reconnect.

Sharing meals was definitely important, a positive step in bringing Will and Harry together. What better time and place to start a good habit than now, at Golden Spurs? She'd do her best to persuade Will of that.

When she emerged from the bathroom it was time to wake the boy. She opened his door and peeked in. He'd burrowed under the covers, and only the crown of his blond head showed. By a lucky stroke of nature, early-morning sunlight squeezed through a crack in the drapes and struck his hair, turning it golden.

The golden-haired son, she thought, smiling. Walking to the bed, she gently pulled back the covers. "Rise and shine, sweetie."

"Mom?" he mumbled, his eyes still shut.

That single word, uttered so sleepily, pierced Dena's heart like a jagged arrow. She ached for this sweet, motherless boy who obviously missed his mother. Right then she fell in love with him. Her resolve to help him tightened.

"No, honey, it's Dena," she replied softly. "Time to get up. We've got to eat breakfast and head for that riding lesson. Get dressed, okay?"

She waited until he sat up and rubbed his eyes, then left him alone and headed toward the cabin's tiny kitchen. The aroma of fresh coffee floated through the air. So Will was up.

Dena saw him before he saw her. Barefoot, in a navy T-shirt and snug, faded jeans, his hair still wet from the shower and slicked back, he looked completely different from the business-attired man of yesterday. Yet like yesterday, utterly male and devastatingly handsome.

As she entered the kitchen, the corner of his mouth quirked sexily. "Morning." His voice was rough with sleep, but his eyes were warm and alert.

"Good morning." Her traitorous pulse shot up. She focused on the coffeepot as she entered the room. "Is that coffee?"

"Sure is. Want some?"

"Please." She couldn't help staring as he opened a cabinet, reached for a mug and set it on the small wood table in front of her. Broad shoulders filled his T-shirt. Tucked neatly into his jeans, it emphasized a flat belly and narrow hips. Below that, a healthy bulge. Swallowing, she jerked her attention upward, to his face.

His eyes glinted, and one brow arched. "Did I pass the test?"

"Wh-what?" Heat prickled her face.

"You were checking me out." He cocked a hip against the counter and crossed his arms. "Now it's my turn."

His gaze raked slowly and thoroughly over her. Suddenly she was too warm, and the room was too small. Snatching the mug from the table, she spun away and reached for the coffeepot. With shaky hands she filled her cup and composed herself. Focusing on her drink, she again faced him. The coffee tasted strong and rich, the way she liked it. "This is very good," she said, watching the steam.

"Thanks."

For a few blessed moments, they shared the silence. Then Will fixed her with an appraising stare. "Why do you dress like that?"

The question sounded like something Reese would have said in his continual quest to mold her into his idea of the perfect wife. Dena cupped her mug and frowned. Maybe she'd misunderstood. "What did you say?"

"Most women with your looks would want to show off what they had." His gaze flickered over her. "What does your boyfriend think of those baggy clothes?"

She hadn't misunderstood. Will was just like Reese. He valued appearance above all. Disappointed but not surprised, she lifted her chin. "I don't have a boyfriend, and I'm not most women."

Will lifted his hands, palms up. "Hey, no need to get defensive." His eyes glinted as they searched hers. "What are you afraid of, Dena?"

His jaw snapped shut, as if his own question astonished him. It certainly surprised Dena. She shifted nervously and stared into her coffee. Through the open window the breakfast chimes tolled. *Saved by the bell.* She set down her cup. "It's time for breakfast. I hope you're planning to eat with Harry and me."

Will held her with his gaze a moment longer. "Of course." He glanced at this watch. "Where is he?"

"Right here." Harry's booted footsteps clipped over the tile floor.

"Good morning." Dena smiled.

Will tipped his mug. "Morning, son. Do those new boots feel all right?"

The boy glanced down self-consciously at the pristine black leather. "Yeah."

"They sure look good," Dena said. Hand on her hip, she took in the dark-brown cowboy hat, jeans, denim shirt with its new creases still intact and silver belt buckle. "In fact, you look just like a real cowboy."

"I do?" Harry brightened, then seemed to catch himself. His expression sobered. "I mean, oh."

Dena stifled a triumphant grin. Already the boy had started to loosen up. In no time at all she'd earn his trust.

If only dealing with his father could be so easy.

Dena needed a hat, Will thought as he stood under the bright morning sun by the horse corral. And she could do with boots and jeans and a shirt that weren't old and two sizes too big. He remembered the way her eyes flashed in anger when he'd asked about her clothes. What had happened to make her want to hide that God-given beauty? Some jerk must have really done a number on her.

His jaw clenched at the thought. He quickly dismissed it. What did her past matter, as long as she took care of Harry?

Still… *I'm not most women,* she'd said. He shook his head. She sure as hell wasn't. He'd never met a female like her. She drove him crazy, telling him in that schoolteacher tone what she thought he should do about Harry. It was none of her damn business.

Yet she intrigued him.

Angled against the freshly painted barn, he studied her. No matter how loose and ugly the clothes, she couldn't hide her attributes. Not from him or any other red-blooded male. Just as in the dining room the night before, men preened and jockeyed around her like teenage boys after the prom queen, while their wives eyed them suspiciously. Will didn't like it, either, but he couldn't fault any of their husbands.

From the corral, several horses nickered impatiently, swishing their tails as they stood in the warm sunshine and waited for their saddles and riders. His thoughts on Dena, Will barely noticed the activity. Most women doted on male attention, but she seemed uncomfortable when a man looked at her. With that pursed mouth she looked disapproving and even prudish.

But he'd seen her eyes warm and her cheeks color, hinting at the fire and passion hidden beneath the surface. He pictured her hungry and aroused. What would that mouth look like then? His blood heated at the image of those lips, kiss swollen and parted, as she lay naked and flushed with longing beneath him.

Damn. With effort he shoved away the vision. Bad enough that he'd lain in bed half the night fantasizing. This morning, listening to her pad down the hall to the bathroom, had been even worse. He'd heard the shower and imagined her, naked under the spray, her breasts beaded with water…

His groin stirred. Double damn. That line of thinking would only lead to trouble. He'd best get rid of those thoughts right now.

Laughter pulled his attention toward the thirty or so kids and adults grouped at the fence, watching half a dozen cowboys, including Foreman Bob from last night, saddle up the horses. A red-haired boy Harry's age stood between his parents, pointing at the animals and shouting excitedly. Harry hovered shyly to one side, his eyes glued to the corral, yet looking very much like he wanted to talk to the boy.

Will's chest tightened. He wanted the kid to make friends.

By the look on Dena's face, so did she. Unlike Will, she seemed to know how to help. He watched as she dropped her arm casually across his son's shoulders and said something Will couldn't hear. Whatever it was, the wariness eased from Harry's expression. The red-headed kid nodded, moved in closer, and began an animated conversation.

Dena's proximity seemed to bolster Harry's confidence, and after a slight hesitation he joined in. Wearing a satisfied smile, she stepped away as if to keep from interfering, but stayed close enough to rescue him if needed.

Gratitude filled Will. Her meddlesome ways drove him crazy, but she possessed a gentle sensitivity his son needed. Maybe this trip would work out after all.

If he could just stop fantasizing about taking her to bed...

"All right, junior ranchers!" Foreman Bob pushed the wide brim of his cowboy hat off a forehead already beaded with sweat, and glanced at the flawless blue sky. Then he turned toward the group. "You ready to ride?"

"Yes!" chorused the children.

"Moms and Dads?"

A significant number replied affirmatively.

The foreman began dividing the riders into small clusters, calling their names and the names of their horses one by one. A male or female cowboy assigned to each group helped the riders mount, adjusted their stirrups and gave instructions about how to sit and how to hold and work the reins. Group by group, horse by horse, they ambled out the gate.

How much longer? Will glanced at his watch. He was due to make that first conference call soon, but first he wanted to see Dena and his son mount their horses and start down the trail.

Finally, when only six people remained, Foreman Bob gestured to include all of them. "The rest of you are going with me. Harry and Dena, meet Ted and Bonnie Williams and their kids, Chad and Emmy."

Harry and his new friend strode eagerly into the corral. Dena and the boy's mother, father and little sister followed more slowly.

This close to the horses, Harry's confident grin faltered. While Chad climbed without hesitation onto a stool in order to reach the stirrup and mount his horse, Dena ruffled Harry's hair and whispered in his ear.

Whatever she said seemed to help. With a sober nod he mimicked his friend's actions. Soon Harry sat astride an enormous fawn-colored horse. A gentle horse, Foreman Bob assured loudly enough for Will to hear.

The boy's face was pale and his mouth pinched,

and he looked vulnerable and very small atop that horse. But he sat straight and proud. A determined glint flashed in his eyes.

Pride rolled through Will. Fear wasn't going to stop his son.

Dena was the last to mount. Bob helped her up, his gaze lingering on her behind. Will scowled.

"How do those stirrups feel?" Bob asked.

She surveyed her feet with a wrinkled brow. "I think they're too long."

The cowboy adjusted them. "Try them now." He watched closely. "Bend your knees and point your toes forward, like this." He placed one hand on her knee. The other circled her ankle.

From Will's view, Bob held on longer than necessary. Will's eyes narrowed. He didn't like the foreman's over-friendly attitude, and he hated the way his grin widened when he looked up at Dena.

He didn't care much for her answering smile, either.

Gripping the fence, Will called out, "When are you coming back?"

"Around lunchtime. We'll go out again at two if the group wants to." The foreman's gaze fastened on Dena.

"Yeah!" the kids exclaimed unanimously.

"Sign me up," Will said before he could stop himself.

"After lunch?" Bob nodded. "Sure thing."

The horses walked single file through the gate. Harry let go of the saddle horn long enough to manage a small wave, then followed the other riders slowly down a sandy trail that cut through the cacti and brush. Dena rode behind the boy, her forehead scrunched in concentration. She shot Will a quick, pleased smile that coaxed a grin from him despite his dark mood. The group soon disappeared in a cloud of dust.

Will headed for the cabin shaking his head. Ride a horse? Crazy, that's what he was. And far too busy to ride. What had gotten into him?

He could always back out. He thought about Dena with that damned cowboy, and bristled. He wanted to make sure the man kept his eye on Harry, not Dena. The only way to do that was to be there.

"That's why I'm going," he muttered to the walkway, to convince himself. Dammit, he couldn't back out now.

Besides, the ride lasted only a couple of hours, on a trained, gentle horse. How difficult could it be?

She'd be good and sore tomorrow, Dena realized. This morning's ride had seemed slow and easy. Still, once she dismounted, thigh muscles she didn't even know she had, twinged and trembled. Now, after a break for lunch, she was back in the saddle. Her legs and bottom protested, aching. Striving for relief, she shifted forward, but that didn't work.

The Williams family had wisely opted for a different activity this afternoon. How had they managed to coax Chad away, and why hadn't Harry and Dena gone with them?

Because of the man on the horse behind her. Will. When he'd decided to ride this afternoon, Harry's face had lit up along with Dena's hopes. Who knew what had changed the man's mind? Maybe the smell of the horses and saddle leather or Harry's excitement. Whatever the reason, Will's change of heart surprised and pleased her.

She glanced back at him. He nodded, but his grim, determined expression remained firmly in place. He looked as if he was in pain. Dena sympathized as she turned her attention back to the trail ahead. Riding wasn't as easy as it looked. Yet Will seemed to know what he was doing.

In boots, faded jeans and a forest-green plaid shirt, riding a large, ebony horse, he easily could have passed for a cowboy. He was one of those men heart-thuddingly handsome in both jeans and custom-made suits. Dena's breath lifted on a romantic sigh. She caught herself and frowned. Straightening, she forced her wayward thoughts to the sand-packed trail that stretched out along the hills and bends of the land.

Foreman Bob reined in his horse, stopped and turned the animal to face them. He said something to Harry. Though Dena's horse was just behind the boy, she couldn't hear the words. Whatever they were, Harry whooped and laughed.

Despite her sore muscles, she couldn't help smiling. It was worth the discomfort to see the boy happy.

With a wink at Harry, the cowboy nodded to Dena. "Harry's doing great." He scrutinized her from the top of her head to her toes. "How about you, little lady?"

"Her name's *Dena,*" Will corrected gruffly.

Dena glanced around at him, her mouth open. His dark eyes were narrowed menacingly at the cowboy. Was he trying to ruin the afternoon? Shooting him a scowl, she turned to the cowboy and smiled.

"I'm having a wonderful time, thank you," she said, ignoring the twinge in her thigh.

"I'll just bet you are," Will muttered.

With a satisfied nod, Bob lowered his reins, then turned his horse. He resumed a slow, easy walk down the trail.

"Let's go, Butter," Harry urged his horse. Dena and her mare followed. From behind, she heard the *clip-clop* of Will's horse and the creak of his saddle.

The hot afternoon sun felt good on her head and shoulders, though she wished she'd worn a hat. She was fair-skinned and burned easily, but hadn't thought to pack one. At least she'd brought and applied a liberal dose of sunblock.

Again Bob reined to a stop and faced the group. "Do you folks feel comfortable enough to try a short lope?"

"Yes!" Harry cried in a voice laced with excitement.

"What's a lope?" Will asked, echoing Dena's unspoken question.

"It's faster than a trot and slower than a run, and a real easy gait to sit. How 'bout it?" Lifting a brow, Bob awaited an answer.

Harry shifted in his saddle and stared at her and Will, his face alive with hope.

Will shrugged. "I'm game."

The idea of moving faster than a walk made Dena's palms go damp. But she couldn't let Harry down. And Will wanted to try it. "Um, sure," she replied brightly.

"All right, then, here's what you do." Bob explained how to lean forward in the saddle and ride with the gait, and how to slow down, then stop. The directions sounded easy enough. When everyone understood, the cowboy pushed his hat down hard on his head. "Let's try it."

He kicked his horse. Suddenly they were off. Dena bounced like a tennis ball, miserably uncomfortable, until the ride suddenly smoothed from a jarring gait to a gentle rocking chair motion. This was more comfortable, but faster. Too fast. Swallowing, she gripped the horse with her knees and hung on tight.

Finally Bob's horse slowed, then stopped. Thankfully the other horses followed his lead. Again he turned his big, black animal. "That's the lope. Did you like it?"

"Cool," Harry said. "Can we do it again?"

Dena brushed the dust out of her eyes. Behind her, Will mumbled something unintelligible in a tone that matched her overwrought state. For Harry, she managed a shaky smile and a nod.

Bob touched the brim of his hat. "We'll go again, as soon as we come to a flat part in the path."

A long time from now, Dena hoped, while Will swore under his breath.

They headed forward. All too soon Bob called out, "Ready?" and kicked his horse.

Dust flew up, stinging Dena's eyes, and grit flew into her open mouth. Hanging on so tightly made her hands ache. She rode blindly, waiting for the trot to turn into a canter. Suddenly her horse veered off the trail, running so fast, the scrub and cacti on either side blurred.

"Stop!" she shrieked, gripping the reins and pulling back. Nothing happened. "Please, stop," she pleaded.

The horse thundered on. Her heart pounded. Dear Lord, she was going to fall, to die. In the desert, with a man and boy she barely knew. "Help!" she yelled, hardly hearing her own shrill scream.

Then, magically, Will was galloping beside her.

"Whoa," he commanded, his voice bouncing. With one hand, he grabbed her reins and pulled.

Her horse jerked to the left, and her foot flew from the stirrup. Off balance, she tilted dangerously.

"We're going down," Will shouted, just as she screamed.

He hit the ground with a thud. Somehow she landed on him.

The horses ran ahead, coming to a stop ten feet away.

"Omigosh," Dena gasped, and tried to untangle her trembling limbs from Will's. Adrenaline shot through her veins, making her breathless and heightening every nerve in her body.

"You all right?" Grasping her shoulders, Will searched her face, his deep, brown eyes probing. Concern filled his expression. For her.

"I think so." Beneath her, his body was hard and warm. She should get up now, but her legs were shaking too hard. "What about you?"

"Fine, except for my pride."

His eyes twinkled, and her pulse leaped. She smiled weakly. "You saved me, Will. Thank you."

"I never could resist a damsel in distress," he teased.

A beat later his eyes turned that warm, chocolaty

brown, and her heartbeat shifted from fear to…an entirely different feeling. Her heart rate quickened. Beneath her palms she felt the matching rhythm of Will's heart.

A deep, warm sound, like a lion's purr, came from his throat. Her bones turned to water. Suddenly she wanted him to kiss her. His gaze wandered to her lips, and she knew he wanted the same thing. His hand slid to the back of her neck. One brow raised in question.

"Yes," she whispered, neither knowing nor caring what she agreed to.

At that moment Bob rode up in a cloud of dust and quickly dismounted. "You folks all right?" he asked, hurrying toward them.

No. Scrambling from Will's arms, Dena managed to push to her feet. Her face prickled with embarrassment. "Fine," she stated, furiously tugging down her shirt.

Harry, white-faced and wild-eyed, rode up behind them. "What happened?"

Will stood and brushed the dust off his rear end. His tight, very nice rear end. Swallowing, Dena turned away.

"For some reason Dena's horse took off," he said. "I went after her."

"But you've never ridden before." Harry's eyes were filled with awe and respect.

To Dena's surprise, Will flushed. He shifted his weight, then shrugged. "I did what I had to do."

Bob frowned. "That was dangerous and reckless. You could have hurt yourself and Dena. The horse would have slowed down soon enough on his own."

Bristling, Will settled his hands low on his hips. "How in hell did I know that? Dena called for help and I—"

"I'm glad Will stopped my horse," she cut in. The last thing they needed was an argument between the two men. She shot Will a grateful smile. "But don't worry, it'll never happen again."

Will scowled and sent a challenging look at the foreman, who pretended not to notice. "The important thing is, you're both okay. Let's call it a day. Mount up and we'll head back."

Limbs trembling, Dena managed to seat herself. She didn't feel "okay." She needed a nice, long soak in the tub and time to pull herself together before dinner. After what had happened, a long, *cold* soak.

She'd almost lost her head, almost kissed Will.

That scared her twice as much as the runaway horse. The fall must have knocked out her common sense. If not for Bob showing up when he did...

She swallowed back that heart-racing train of thought. She was all right now, once again in her right mind. Nothing like this would ever happen again, she was sure of it. Relieved, she loosened her grip on the reins and let the horse lead her back to the corral.

Chapter Four

Wincing with each step, Dena slowly made her way into the tiny kitchen the next morning. Every muscle in her body ached. Even her skin hurt, but that was because the sunblock hadn't worked. Her face, ears and neck were the color of a grilled salmon. Sunburned and sore, she longed to crawl carefully back into bed with a good book. But that wasn't part of her job description.

Besides, she'd promised to ride with Harry this morning. She groaned at the thought. A few more hours in the saddle might cripple her for life, and who knew if the new tube of sunblock would save her skin from further abuse? At least he'd agreed to try a different activity after lunch.

Though Dena badly needed coffee, she hesitated just outside the kitchen. Will stood at the small window, his back to her. She hadn't seen him since dinner the night before.

After eating he'd returned to the cabin to work, while she'd explored the main lodge with Harry. Later, when the boy went to bed, Will had retreated into his room. Dena hadn't minded. She'd needed solitude to sort out her thoughts.

They fled as she studied Will from behind. Freshly pressed slacks hung nicely from his narrow hips. A burgundy golf shirt hugged his broad shoulders and set off skin bronzed by yesterday's afternoon in the sun. He was one of those lucky men who tanned instead of burned.

Unaware of her, he lifted his hands overhead and stretched. For some reason her heart kicked up a notch. Sternly ignoring the sudden fluttering in her stomach, she strode into the room, brisk and businesslike, though muscles everywhere twinged painfully. "Good morning."

"Morning." His gaze flickered over her, then away, as if he, too, wanted to avoid contact. "Coffee?"

His fingers brushed hers as he handed her a mug. It was only a brief, accidental touch. Yet heat shimmered between them like the steam rising from their drinks. Interest flared in his eyes.

The flush of pleasure that washed over Dena unnerved her. Dropping her gaze to the diamond-patterned linoleum, she backed away until the counter stopped her.

Distance didn't help. She needed to get away from him, from herself. She glanced toward the door. "I'd better wake Harry."

"It's early yet, let him sleep awhile longer. I want to talk to you." He paused to sip his coffee. "We've been in Arizona a day and a half now. What's your take on Harry? Does he like it here?"

Dena was eager to discuss the boy. "He seems to. Last night we found a game room in the lodge, not far from the dining room. He played pool with Chad and some of the other kids." She thought about Harry's buoyant chatter and smiled. "I think he enjoyed himself."

"So he's making friends." Will nodded approvingly. "That's good."

"And he loves the horses. He had a great time riding with you yesterday, Will."

His mouth quirked. "Also good."

"Are you coming with us this morning?"

He shook his head. "I've got to finish some paperwork and fax it to Cal, then set up an appointment with a couple of potential business associates who live in Phoenix."

Dena ignored the disappointment that skated through her. "Harry's going to miss you."

"He's got friends now." Will tipped his mug toward her. "And you. He'll be fine."

"Can't the paperwork wait? You're the one he needs, Will. I really think you should come with us."

"I'll keep that in mind, but we're at a crucial point in negotiations for that land deal." He crossed his arms. "I'm sticking by the phone."

His jaw set stubbornly, and she knew arguing was pointless. She threw up her hands. "All right, then, it'll be just Harry, me and Bob."

"Bob?" Will frowned. "I don't trust him. Find another guide."

"Why? He's great with kids, and Harry likes him."

His expression blank, Will regarded her. "Do you?"

"He's a good riding instructor, if that's what you mean. Beyond that, I hadn't thought about it."

Her response seemed to satisfy him. He nodded. "Fair enough." Abruptly he switched topics. "Did you enjoy the ride yesterday?"

"Well…" Dena tried to think about her horse, the magic of the wide-open spaces and the warmth of the sun on her shoulders. Instead she recalled the feel of Will's solid body beneath her and his arms wrapped protectively around her. And those heart-melting eyes locked on her face.

Those same eyes, cooler now, peered intently at her, and again she felt as if they could see into her. She brushed a nonexistent crumb from the counter. "I liked riding, except for that fall." She tried a smile. "I'm a little sore today, though. And I'll probably be worse this afternoon."

Will's mouth quirked as he rubbed his hip. "I wasn't going to admit it, but I'm sore, too."

The grin transformed his face. Dena's heart flip-flopped. She smiled back. "You hit the ground hard. And when I landed on you—"

"The whole thing scared the hell out of me," Will replied, and Dena wasn't sure if he meant the fall or what had almost happened between them.

His gaze lit on her mouth, and she knew he was remembering the electricity that had arced between them. He swallowed and raised his eyes to her face. "I may never be the same."

Tell me about it. Flustered, she pulled her attention to the mug cupped in her hands. "They say getting right back on is the way to conquer your fears." She sipped. "Come with us, Will."

"I'm not afraid." He scowled and set his mug in the sink. "Just busy."

She gazed up at the white stucco ceiling and shook her head. "I tried." Wincing, she gingerly touched her neck. "Darned sunburn."

"That reminds me, I've got something for you." Will gestured toward the living room. "In here."

Curious, she followed him.

"I found this at the gift shop." He picked up a cream-color cowboy hat and handed it to her. "For you," he said roughly.

"Me?" His thoughtfulness surprised and pleased her. "Thank you." She turned the hat around in her hands. Stetson, the brand read. Dollar signs rolled through her head. "But I can't accept this."

"Sure you can. The Arizona sun is deadly even in early April, and you need to protect that pretty face. Think of it as necessary equipment for taking Harry riding. I guessed at the size. Let's see how it fits."

Tugging the hat from her hands, he set it on her head, then angled it. He was so close she felt his breath on her face, smelled his woodsy cologne.

"There." His expression warmed as he stepped back. "Now you're a bona fide cowgirl. Take a look."

Breathless, as if she'd run a mile, Dena moved toward the living room mirror. Were her cheeks flushed from too much sun or something else? She tilted her head this way and that, admiring her reflection. The hat fitted perfectly.

She smiled. "Well, since it'll keep the sun off my face... But I'm going to pay you back." Though it would take half a paycheck.

"No need for that." He dismissed the offer with a gesture. "Taking good care of my son is payback enough." His voice was gruff and his expression neutral, but his eyes lit softly. "I appreciate what you're doing for him, Dena."

"Thank you. And thanks for this wonderful hat." Without thinking she stood on her toes and kissed his cheek. His freshly shaved face was smooth and warm beneath her lips. Up close like this he smelled even better, a mix of cologne and his own unique scent.

Before she could pull away, he cupped her upper arms and studied her face through heavy-lidded eyes. A low groan broke from his throat.

Her breath caught. He was going to do it now, kiss her. Heaven help her, she wanted that. She lifted her face in unspoken reply. His lips brushed softly over hers, teasing. Suddenly he released her.

Cool air filled the space vacated by his body. Dena opened her eyes, which had somehow closed. She watched his chest as it rose and fell rapidly. Somewhere in the distance a door opened and footsteps padded down the hall.

"I'm sorry—"

"I didn't mean—"

They began at the same time.

"Dena?" Harry called. "Where are you?"

Will cleared his throat. "In here with me," he replied, without taking his eyes from her. "I shouldn't have done that," he said in a low voice. "It won't happen again."

"No, it won't." Embarrassed, she bit her lip. What had gotten into her? She was Harry's nanny, for goodness sake. Besides, she didn't want to kiss Will Stoner.

Harry entered the room, and she turned toward him, glad for the diversion. By the time they headed for breakfast, she'd managed to calm her racing heart.

What had happened was a mistake. Thank goodness Will understood that. Thank goodness they understood each other.

If only she understood herself as well.

Squealing children, splashing water, and the sound of tinkling ice cubes filled the poolside air. Dena smiled lazily as she lounged under a large beach umbrella near the pool. Thankfully Harry had settled on swimming this afternoon. Physically exhausted and still undone by her brazen behavior this morning, she welcomed a chance to simply relax.

Beside her, Bonnie Williams twirled a frosty glass of cola. When Harry had decided to swim after the morning horseback ride, Chad and Emmy had enthusiastically followed suit. Their father had opted to play golf, but Bonnie and the kids had joined Dena and Harry for a poolside lunch and swim.

Dena liked Bonnie, her husband Ted and their children. If they lived in the same town, she and Bonnie might become close friends. But the Williamses lived in New York, on the opposite side of the country.

"Mommy, Chad's splashing me," five-year-old Emmy whined, rubbing her eyes.

"Emmy's about ready for a nap," Bonnie said in a low voice. Frowning, she leaned forward, pushing her sunglasses to the top of her curly red hair. "Chad Williams, stop splashing your sister."

The boy rolled his big blue eyes. "Come on, Harry, let's see if we can swim all the way across, underwater."

"Yeah." Harry nodded and grabbed the side of the pool. "We're each allowed three deep breaths first, okay?" He turned to Emmy, whose lower lip puffed out sadly. "You watch, Emmy, and make sure nobody cheats."

The pout disappeared into a dimpled grin. "'Kay."

Bonnie glanced at Dena before slipping her sunglasses back on. "He's so sweet to include her."

"Thank you." Dena smiled at this new side of Harry. Who'd have guessed that buried under that big chip on his shoulder lurked such a thoughtful, kind boy? She hoped to see lots more of what she suspected was his true nature. And would, in due time. All he needed was love, trust and patience. She redoubled her commitment to give him all three and to encourage Will to give the same.

"I wish Chad treated Emma like that," Bonnie continued. "I swear, all they do is fight. Is that normal?"

Dena had told her about pursuing a degree in child psychology. She picked up her lemonade and nodded. "Of course. If Harry had a sister, I'm sure he'd argue with her, too."

"Maybe someday he will." The redhead's brow arched knowingly.

Dena's glass froze halfway to her mouth. "What do you mean?"

"You and Will, what else?" Bonnie knew about Harry's mother and evidently had jumped to a few erroneous conclusions.

To Dena's chagrin, her face heated. "Wait a minute. I'm Harry's nanny, and that's it. Will and I aren't—we don't…" Flustered, she tried again. "Under my employment contract, anything else would be unethical and grounds for termination. Besides, Will's not interested. And neither am I."

She refused to think about what had happened this morning. That had been a mistake, as had the near kiss after the riding mishap. Two mistakes in two days. She frowned.

Bonnie pooh-poohed the objections with a wave. "You know, I started out as Ted's secretary. One look at the man, and I was a goner." She sighed dreamily. "It took me three years, but I finally got him to ask me out. Eight months later, we were married. It's going on ten years now, and we're more in love than ever. Plus we've got two wonderful kids." She eyed Dena over her sunglasses. "It could be the same with you and Will. He's a successful, good-looking man, and you're beautiful. And it's obvious you're crazy about Harry. Why not?"

Dena had always wanted children, but that was a lost dream, as was finding love. She shook her head. "I tried marriage once before to a man like Will, but it didn't work out."

From day one, Reese had tried to make her into

someone she wasn't. Because she'd been young and naive and full of ideas about love and marriage, and because her ailing parents liked Reese, she'd tried to change, setting aside her dream of a psychology degree and dressing in the tight, sexy clothes he selected. She'd dropped all her male friends because he'd demanded it. He'd rewarded her by belittling her efforts and sleeping with other women. And giving her a divorce only when she agreed to take nothing from the marriage but her clothes and the things she'd owned before the marriage. She suppressed a shudder. Thank goodness her parents hadn't lived long enough to see their dreams for her shatter. "I don't want to make the same mistake twice."

At that moment Emmy's loud wail rang out. Bonnie stood up. "I'd love to talk more about this, but I'm afraid she's past due for that nap." She plucked her daughter from the water and deftly wrapped her in a towel.

On cue, Ted strode toward her, pulling his golf clubs behind him. "Miss me?" The tall, lanky man kissed his wife soundly.

"Gross," Chad grumbled from the pool, though his cockeyed grin belied the words. He turned to Harry, who watched the affectionate adults with interest. "They're always doing that kissy-face stuff."

Ted released his breathless wife and hunkered down beside the pool. "Hey, boys." He grinned. "I'm going to borrow Chad for a while, okay Harry?" He ruffled his son's wet hair. "I rented us a bicycle built for two. How about you get dressed?"

"Cool." The boy beamed and dog-paddled to the ladder.

The longing that filled Harry's face was difficult to miss. He no doubt yearned for the same kind of attention from Will. Dena's heart contracted. She wanted to hug the boy in a comforting embrace, but that would embarrass him. Instead she held out a towel. "Time to get out, kiddo."

"Okay." He climbed up the ladder without a trace of his earlier exuberance.

Bonnie scooped up her exhausted daughter. "Bye Dena, bye, Harry. We'll probably see you after dinner, in the game room."

"See you tonight, Harry," Chad echoed over his shoulder.

His expression sober, Harry watched them walk away.

"You need more sunblock." Dena beckoned him down beside her and squirted a generous glob of lotion into her palm. It was warm from the sun. "All this sitting around has made me hungry. You must be starved. How about an ice cream cone? Two scoops if you want."

He shrugged listlessly.

"I thought you loved ice cream." She began to rub the warm sunblock over his narrow shoulders. "What's the matter, sweetie?"

"Nothing." He stared at his water-shriveled toes.

Dena bit her lip, wondering how to coax him into opening up. Maybe if she started first... "My mom and dad never expected to have children," she said, running her palms slowly over his back. "Then one day, when they were almost old enough to be grandparents, I came along. You can bet *that* was a surprise."

Harry's head angled, and she knew she had his attention.

"All my friends' parents were young, like Chad's," she continued. "They hiked together, went swimming and took vacations to exciting places. But my parents didn't do any of that. It made me feel lonely."

Harry looked over his shoulder at her. "What did you do?"

"Well, I knew my mom and dad loved me. So one day I decided to tell them how I felt." She squirted more lotion into her hand. "They listened carefully. A few days later my father brought home a pair of secondhand roller skates. We didn't have much money for new ones. He and my mother had met at a roller-skating party. They hadn't skated for years, but they took me to a rink and taught me what they knew. We had a wonderful time." She rubbed a last smear of lotion into Harry's nape. "They said they hadn't understood and thanked me for showing them how to be young again. After that, whenever I had a worry or problem, I talked to them about it." She let out a wistful sigh. "They're both dead now. I sure do miss them and the good times we had together."

Harry didn't reply, so Dena handed him the sunblock. "Put some on your legs."

He did. After a few moments he bowed his head. "Will would never take me bike riding."

"He's never had a son before, Harry. Maybe if you asked him…" She let the words trail off.

"It won't do any good. He doesn't want me. He never has."

Dena couldn't see the boy's eyes, but his voice was

filled with such pain and despair that her heart ached for him. She renewed her vow to help father and son come together. Pretending to rub in a missed dab of sunblock, she touched his shoulder reassuringly. "That's not true."

"My mom said so, and she wouldn't lie. Will got stuck with me when she died."

Will had told Dena a similar story, but had seemed disappointed, angry even, not "stuck." She shook her head. "Then your mom made a mistake. I happen to know your dad cares a whole lot about you."

Harry scowled as he raised his head. "If that's true, then why are *you* here?"

The question meant to sting and it did, like a slap across the face. Undaunted, she calmly explained. "This is a working vacation for your dad, remember? That's why I came along on this trip, so you could have some fun. And while we're out here swimming, he's inside slaving away. I feel sorry for him, don't you?"

A thought crossed her mind that maybe she'd approached the problem with Will and Harry from the wrong angle. Waiting and hoping for Will to join in the fun wasn't working.

No, it was up to her to bring them together. And she would, starting now. She'd sign the three of them up for several activities, then tell Will after the fact. He couldn't very well back out of that.

Pleased with her solution, she grinned and stuffed the lotion and Harry's swimming goggles into her bag. "Come on." She stood and reached out a hand. "Let's get those ice cream cones. We'll buy one for your dad, too. I'll bet you anything he'll love it."

She would personally slit his throat if he didn't.

"Yeah, right," Harry mumbled, but he let her pull him up.

She rejoiced privately at the tiny gesture of trust. It wasn't much, but it was a start.

"A Jeep canyon ride *when?*" Will set down his dessert fork and stifled a groan. All he wanted was to finish dinner in peace, return to the cabin and get back to work.

"Tomorrow," Dena replied, demurely wiping her mouth. "We leave at one and drive to Vulture Mine Canyon, stopping along the way for short side trips."

"We might even see a coyote or wild rabbits," Harry added. His eyes sparkled with excitement as never before. Since he'd surprised Will with ice cream this afternoon, the boy had seemed happier and more at ease.

Will grinned at this new, talkative side of his son. "That sounds exciting."

He cast a grateful nod at Dena. In a matter of days, thanks to her, things had definitely changed for the better. He owed her a lot. If things continued the way they were going, she'd end up with an extended contract and a raise.

She smiled and picked up where she'd left off. "We'll return to the ranch in plenty of time for dinner. It's the perfect setup, Will. You can work before and after."

Will glanced from Dena to Harry. Both regarded him expectantly. He was about to disappoint them, but it couldn't be helped. He held out his hands. "I'd like to, but Cal's on the verge of closing that land deal. I need to stick close to the phone. You'll have to go without me.''

Harry's mouth compressed. Disappointment shadowed his face as he stared down at his plate.

Will felt like a jerk, but what choice did he have? This was an important deal. He couldn't just walk away for half the day. Nor did he want to.

Dena frowned. ''You have to come with us, Will. I signed you up. Bring your cell phone, if you must. Better yet, can't Cal handle the business by himself for one day?''

''Not tomorrow, and what if the phone can't pick up where we're going?'' Will glanced at his son, hoping to make him understand. ''Maybe another time.''

Dena shook her head. ''The only Jeep ride scheduled is for tomorrow. We're signed up for a cookout the day after that and the following morning, a hot-air-balloon ride. I reserved spaces for all three of us, Will.''

He frowned. ''You *what?*''

''They're nonrefundable,'' she added, and, lifting a brow, waited expectantly.

Well, hell. Seconds ticked by as he considered how to respond.

''Told you, Dena.'' Abruptly Harry pushed back his chair. ''I'm going to the game room to find Chad.''

Will's spirits sank. He jumped up. ''Wait a minute, son.''

''Stay away from me.'' Harry shot him a murderous glance, then ran through the spacious dining room and out the door.

Curious diners glanced at Will. He shrugged and

sank onto his chair with an exasperated sigh. "What'd I do?"

Dena's mouth opened, then shut. "You're really clueless, aren't you?"

He squeezed the bridge of his nose. "Try to understand, Dena. I grew up dirt poor. I didn't even know luxury like this," he gestured at the room, "existed. I spent my days taking care of my brother and worrying about how we were going to eat. Because of my successful business, Harry will never have to worry about any of those things."

"Some things are more important than success and money." Her lips pursed disapprovingly. "You're a workaholic, Will."

"You say that as if it's a curse."

Her brows arched. "I think it is."

His pride pricked, he snorted. "I built a commercial real estate company from scratch without help from anyone, and earned a fortune along the way. Unfortunately, I lost most of it to my ex-wife." She'd played him like a fool, pretending to love him when all she cared about was his bankroll. "So I rolled up my sleeves and earned it all back again and more. How? Through dedication and hard work."

"What's the point of all that wealth if you never stop to enjoy life? Maybe it's relaxing you're afraid of."

He'd heard that before from his brother. The words had irked him then, and they irked him now. Mark had nothing to show for his laid-back life but the acreage and small bungalow Will had deeded him. Without Will, Mark would live in some seedy apartment. He wouldn't have his current construction job with the company.

Besides, money was straightforward. It didn't play with a man's feelings. "There's nothing more satisfying than building up a healthy bank balance," he said, pausing to loosen his tie. "And believe me, I know how to relax with the best of them. But right now, my company is in the middle of a huge business deal. Cal needs my help, and I won't let him down. I can't."

"What about your son? Harry needs you too, Will."

The sad, accusing look in her eyes hit him harder than any words could. He shifted in his seat. "My business means everything to me. How can I make you understand?"

"Oh, I think I get the picture." Tossing her napkin down, she rose. "I'm going to find Harry."

From his seat at the vacated table, Will watched her hurry from the room. Despite the old, loose-fitting dress, the graceful sway of her hips attracted attention.

His gut knotted. He'd blown it this time.

"Ridiculous," he muttered, shoving a mouthful of lemon meringue pie into his mouth. It tasted like cotton.

In the bar off the dining room, a jazz band tuned up for a night of dancing. A trumpet trilled scales while the deep sounds of a bass twanged in the background.

The upbeat sounds clashed with Will's mood and somehow further lowered his spirits. Frowning, he made his way out of the dining room and into the night. The rapidly cooling air and twinkling path lights supplied little comfort. He headed away from the ranch and onto the golf course, until the sounds faded.

Alone in the darkness he stared up at the starlit sky. He wanted to do the right thing and figured he had. He'd taken in Harry, provided him with a home and the things that were important to a boy. Toys and clothes and good food, things Will had yearned for as a child. Apparently, Harry didn't.

Will released a frustrated breath. What *did* his son want?

Dena's words echoed in his head. *Harry needs you.*

He knew she was right. If he were honest, he would admit that he'd longed for the same thing from his overworked mother. She hadn't been able to spare the time. In fact, she had depended on him to take care of his little brother, Mark. To be a surrogate father to a boy a mere three years younger than he.

A job he'd failed miserably. Mark had been in and out of trouble for most of his thirty years, through a bad marriage and unable to hold a job until recently. Tension climbed up Will's neck as it always did when he thought of how he'd failed Mark. He rolled his shoulders several times. It didn't help.

Now he had to do it all over again, take care of someone. His son. This time with plenty of money. And enough smarts to know he was lousy father material. But dammit, he couldn't give up. This was his son. He didn't want to screw up.

Harry's face flashed before him, the boy's mouth set and his eyes a mixture of disappointment and resentment. Exhaling heavily, Will scrubbed a hand over his face. So far he'd screwed up plenty.

Dena had said that Harry needed him. Maybe so. He had to find a way to be with the boy, he promised himself. Soon. But not now. There was too much riding on this land acquisition.

Besides, more than Harry needed Will, he needed someone who knew how to discipline the boy, knew the right things to do and say. At least for now, that person was Dena. She didn't seem to like Will much, but she doted on the boy. Hiring her had been a good decision. If this trip worked out, maybe he'd employ her permanently.

The thought eased his conscience. Now he could concentrate on the work he must finish tonight, a list of questions and concerns he wanted Cal to read and respond to first thing tomorrow. Turning his thoughts to his business, he strode toward the cabin.

Chapter Five

"Nooooo!"

Harry's terrified scream jerked Will from a restless sleep. His heart pounding, he flipped on the bedside light and blinked in the sudden brightness. Poor kid must have had a nightmare. As he swung his legs over the side of the bed, he heard footsteps pad quickly down the hall and Dena's voice calling out to the boy. Shoving his legs into his pants, he yanked open his door and strode from his room.

Harry's door gaped open. The soft lamplight pouring through it beckoned Will forward. Yet he hesitated, remaining in the dark shadows of the hall. Dena was already in there, doing her job. He didn't want to crowd her.

Yeah, right. The sad truth was, much as he wanted to comfort his son, he didn't know how. Things between him and Harry were bad enough. He wasn't about to make them worse by marching in there and screwing up. Planting his feet firmly where he stood, he peered unseen into the room.

Dena sat perched on the edge of the bed beside the ashen-faced boy. She looked sleep tousled and worried.

"What's the matter, Harry?" she asked in a low, sweet voice that could have warmed the coldest of men.

But this was no man, this was Harry. And he didn't open up to anyone, not even the lovely woman beside him.

His shoulders were hunched in misery, his thin arms folded across his waist. Will could no longer see the small face because Harry's head was bowed. He couldn't hear Harry's reply because he wasn't talking. No surprise there.

"Harry?" Dena prodded, smoothing his hair off his forehead. "You can tell me."

Instead of replying, he stiffened and pressed his lips together. Will tensed. *What now, Dena?*

"Come here, sweetie," she crooned.

For once, her hair was down, tumbling to her shoulders in ripples of blond silk. Her face was filled with caring and concern for the boy. For his son. Will swallowed as a mixture of emotions he didn't understand whirled through him.

Opening her arms, she tugged the kid close. As she did, his face crumpled. Noisy sobs broke from his throat as he sank miserably against her.

"I m-miss my m-mom," he bawled.

Will's chest contracted painfully. At the same time

he was surprised that his son had confided in Dena. He knew how it felt to mourn a parent, and God knew, he hated seeing the boy hurt. But he didn't know how to help.

Dena seemed to know exactly what to say and do. So he stayed where he was and, feeling like a voyeur, watched and listened.

"I know," she murmured as she rocked the boy. "Sometimes it feels better if you talk about it."

Harry sniffled loudly. "Why did she have to d-die?"

Will had asked himself that same unanswerable question, both over the past month and when his own father had died.

Dena bit her lip. "I wish I could answer that, but I can't. No one can." She tipped up the boy's chin and gently blotted away the tears with a tissue. "I know you're sad, sweetie, but at least you've still got your dad."

Thank you, Dena. Will's mouth quirked in silent appreciation. He wanted to stride into the room, gather his son in his arms, and hold him. His eyes on his boy, he moved silently toward the door.

With an angry shake of his head, Harry pulled out of her arms. "Will doesn't like me."

The words cut like a knife. Stung and frustrated, he halted outside the door. He couldn't go in there, not now.

"We talked about this before." Her expression full of pain and sympathy, Dena handed him a fresh tissue from the box on the bedside table. "I happen to know your dad wants and loves you."

Will nodded. Damn straight.

The kid's skeptical look made him flinch. A disconcerted sigh slipped from Dena's lips. "He really does, sweetie. He just doesn't know how to show it."

Will rolled his eyes. A man didn't give his son food, shelter and the best of everything unless he cared. Why couldn't Harry see that? What was he supposed to do, write a poem? He wasn't the kind of man who wore his heart on his sleeve.

"Any man would be proud to call you his son," she continued. "You're a great kid, and I like you a lot." She smiled sadly. "To tell you the truth, I always wanted a child just like you." The heartfelt longing in her voice left no doubt she meant what she said.

Will frowned. She was young, beautiful and healthy, with plenty of time to marry and have a family. So what was the problem?

"If you want a boy like me, why don't you have one?" Harry asked, with an eight-year-old's curiosity and straightforwardness.

Curious himself, Will cocked his head and leaned forward to listen.

Dena sighed and smoothed her white terry robe over her thighs, as if deciding what to say. "The truth is, I used to be married to a man who didn't want children." She lifted her shoulders. "We're divorced now."

Her words surprised Will. She seemed young to have been married and divorced.

"You can always get married again," Harry said.

She shook her head. "As much as I'd love to have kids, I don't think so. Marriage doesn't agree with me."

Will knew exactly how she felt, and he concurred. He'd made a mistake once, thought he'd fallen in love. Scarcely a year into the marriage, he'd learned the bitter truth. She wanted his money and not him. He scowled, remembering how stupid he had felt and how much it had hurt. He'd never again fall into the trap of unholy matrimony.

Dena's marriage must have been as hellish as his. Will shook his head. How could any man give up a woman so beautiful and forthright? Frowning, he quickly dismissed the question. Her past was none of his concern. And he'd heard enough. He should head back to his room now and rest up for tomorrow. Instead he stayed put.

Dena managed a weak smile and tweaked Harry's nose, the movement spreading her robe open at the neck and revealing what looked like a pink cotton T-shirt underneath. "And, anyway, I've got other priorities right now, like taking care of you."

"Hey," Harry said, dipping his head while he fiddled with his tissue, "maybe you could marry Will."

What the—? Will barely managed to cover his surprise.

"Harry!" Dena gasped. An unmistakable flush deepened the pink of her sun-colored cheeks. "Your dad and I...well, I mean, things aren't like that between us. I work for him."

"Oh."

The boy sounded disappointed. Will rubbed the back of his neck. Great. Not only did he have a son who didn't feel wanted, but the boy thought Will should take up with the nanny.

He ignored the fact that his thoughts had run in the

same direction. No, thanks. Hell, he wasn't even looking for a long-term relationship. Running a company and handling his son was responsibility enough. If he couldn't stop thinking about Dena, well, that was lust, pure and simple, and easy to tame.

"That doesn't mean you and I can't be together, right?" she said. "We're a team. Right, kiddo?"

After a moment Harry nodded. "Right."

They exchanged a high five. A beat later the small brow wrinkled with uncertainty. "But you might leave like those other nannies." He hung his head. "They didn't like me."

Will grimaced. No kid should feel unloved, especially his. Hurting for his son, he vowed silently to protect him from further pain. He'd make sure Dena stuck around for a long time.

No matter what it took.

"I'm sure they liked you fine, Harry. And I'm sure their leaving had nothing to do with you." She offered a tender smile guaranteed to bolster the kid's morale. "And hey, I'm still here, aren't I? Trust me, I don't intend to go anywhere." Her chin lifted defiantly, and her chest rose. "If your dad can put up with me."

The movement thrust her ample breasts against her robe. Her hair rippled like waves, hitting just about at nipple level. Fresh unwanted lust shot through Will. His fingers flexed at his sides as he imagined reaching out and combing his hands through that hair, following the silken ends to the jut of her breasts. He would tease the sensitive peaks until her lips parted in a moan and she—

Stifling a groan, he tamped down that train of

thought. He didn't want to think of Dena that way. The damned female was headstrong and far too desirable for her own good, a combination that gave him a giant headache. But Harry liked her. And Will needed her. They both did.

Thank God she wanted to stay.

The boy yawned loudly and sank against the pillows. Dena pulled up the covers and gently tucked them under his chin the way a loving mother would. "It's time to get to sleep. You want to be rested up for the morning ride and that canyon trip tomorrow afternoon, don't you?"

With an odd catch in his throat, Will watched her kiss his son good-night. As she switched off the bedside lamp, Will crept quietly back to his room. If she found him eavesdropping, she'd no doubt purse her lips and once again lecture him on how to raise his son. She'd make him feel like a jerk for standing here instead of joining her in Harry's room.

Will didn't think he could take that, not tonight. Not in that robe, with her hair down and soft around her face.

Weary, he crawled into bed. Tomorrow was an important day for the company. He needed sleep. But thoughts raced through his mind, and it took a long time to settle down.

Finally he bunched his pillow under his head and gave up. He had to do something about Harry. He had to become a better father. He could negotiate complicated real estate deals; surely he could improve his miserable parenting skills.

Starting tomorrow, things were going to change.

The decision eased some of the tension from his gut. Yawning, he rolled over.

All he had to do now was figure out how and what to change.

"We're running late, Harry. Why don't you bring the rest of that sandwich with you?" Dena suggested during lunch the next afternoon. After their morning horseback ride, they'd barely managed enough time to wash up and change into shorts, let alone grab a quick meal.

"I'm done." Harry stuffed the remnants of his chicken-salad sandwich into his mouth and jumped up. He swiped two sugar cookies in one hand and tried to snatch two cans of pop with the other, but his grip wasn't wide enough. At Dena's curious look, he shrugged and swallowed his food. "One's for Chad," he explained.

Since Will wasn't joining them and the tickets were nonrefundable, they'd invited Harry's friend along to keep him company. That way, the seat didn't go to waste.

"Here, I'll help you." Dena relieved him of the drinks and grabbed a chilled bottle of sparkling water for herself. She'd wanted to tell Will about the boy's nightmare in hopes of persuading him to join them. But there'd been no sign of the man this morning, not in the cabin or at breakfast. And the cabin was empty when they returned to change clothes before lunch. No doubt he was in the business center next to the lodge, sending an e-mail or faxing something.

Anything to avoid spending time with his son.

Dena let out a frustrated sigh as they set off for the parking lot.

"What's the matter?" Harry asked, casting a worried glance at her.

"Not a thing." She forced a reassuring smile. Will Stoner was as hardheaded as the concrete walkway, but she wouldn't give up. She squared her shoulders. Eventually he'd realize spending time with Harry was worth more than increasing his fortune. Meantime, she aimed to make this afternoon wonderful for the boy.

They neared the parking lot where a long, green vehicle that looked like a cross between a Jeep and a minivan sat parked and waiting. A small group clustered around it.

"There's Chad!" Harry hurried to greet his friend.

The rest of the Williams clan was there, too, including a sleepy-eyed Emmy. At the sight of Harry, the little girl lit up and moved directly into his path. "Hi, Harry."

"Hi, Em." Despite his excitement to reach his friend, he tore off a chunk of cookie and handed it to her.

Bonnie spotted Dena and waved. Dena waved back. Ted and a tall, lanky, college-age male ambled around from the other side of the van. His Steve's Canyon Ride T-shirt and name badge identified him as Steve. Suddenly another man appeared behind them.

Will. Dena's eyes widened behind her sunglasses. What was he doing here? Last night he'd said he couldn't join them today. In khaki shorts, a rust T-shirt and hiking boots, with an expensive-looking camera dangling from straps around his neck and sporting a pair of sunglasses, he appeared to have changed his mind.

She couldn't help noticing his long legs, flecked with dark hair. For a man who worked at a desk all the time, they were surprisingly tanned and muscled. Was his whole body like that, dark and lean and fit?

"Hello, Dena." She couldn't see his eyes behind the sunglasses, but his mouth quirked.

Caught ogling him. Her face heating, she jerked her gaze upward. "What are *you* doing here? Don't you have that important business deal to worry about?"

He shrugged and shifted his weight as if the question made him uncomfortable. "There's nothing more I can do until Cal finishes the negotiations. I thought I'd join you and Harry."

"That's wonderful." Her heart kicked joyfully, almost too joyfully. Because she was pleased for Harry, she assured herself. "Did you hear that, kiddo?" she called out, smiling. "Your dad's coming with us."

"Oh." The boy's expression brightened a moment, but he quickly sobered. "But we gave Chad the ticket. There might not be enough room."

The pain that flashed across Will's face disappeared before Harry noticed. Dena saw it though, and frowned. The boy wanted his father's attention, but was clearly afraid to let on. The two Stoner males were very much alike, she decided with a sigh.

It was up to her to push them together. She glanced inside the spacious vehicle. "This is a big van, and I'm sure there's plenty of room." She turned to Steve. "Right?"

The guide pulled off his baseball cap, wiped his

forehead, and nodded. "Sure. We'll just add it to the bill. You folks ready to go?" He slid open the heavy side doors and waved at the two benches behind the driver's seat. "I suggest you boys each take a window, so you won't miss anything."

Chattering and laughing, Chad and Harry scrambled up and climbed into the back. As they did, Bonnie pulled Dena aside. "Sure you don't mind if Chad comes along?" she asked in a low voice. "I wouldn't want him to intrude on your family time."

Dena thought about the tension between Will and Harry, and shook her head. "Believe me, he's welcome."

Chad slid open the window and peered out. "Hey, Mom and Dad, what are you going to do while I'm gone and Emmy takes her nap?"

"We'll figure out something," Ted replied. He shared a brief, meaningful look with his wife that left do doubt how they planned to spend their time alone. Making love.

Dena felt Will's gaze on her and glanced at him. They'd both removed their sunglasses, and his eyes glinted with interest. She hadn't made love for a long time, hadn't even wanted to. Yet suddenly her body pulsed with need. Flustered, she turned away and climbed into the middle seat. Will followed. Steve pulled the huge doors shut with a loud clank.

Seat belts clicked shut. From the window Bonnie caught Dena's eye. Nodding her chin in Will's direction, she arched that all-knowing brow. Dena waved and pretended not to notice.

As they drove away from the ranch, Steve turned on his microphone and began a colorful dialogue about the plants and history of the area. "Those tall cacti to your right are called saguaro, and they're Arizona's state flower." He pointed to the stately cacti dotting the hills. "Those tall ones are more than a hundred years old."

"I learned about those on the horse trail," Harry said. "If you cut one down, you have to pay five hundred dollars."

Steve glanced in the rearview mirror and nodded. "That's right."

Beaming proudly, Will glanced over his shoulder, at his son. "I'm impressed, Harry."

The boy didn't reply but his shoulders straightened and his chin lifted.

It wasn't much, but it was a start. Hope blossomed in Dena's chest. Maybe things between them were going to be all right, after all. Will seemed to sense the same thing. Low in the seat, where Harry couldn't see, he gave a thumbs-up sign.

Dena returned the signal. His mouth quirked in that sexy, half grin that caused her pulse to flutter. Happy for the man and his son, she smiled back.

"Look out your side, Dena," Chad shouted. "There are a whole bunch of really tall saguaro on that hill over there."

"Let's see." Will leaned across the seat and peered out her window.

His bare thigh touched hers. The air was hot and his skin warm, yet she shivered. The hair on his leg tickled pleasantly, but she didn't feel like laughing. She wanted to lean against him, to rest her head against his chest. To lift her face and kiss him.

Feeling foolish, she inched away. He'd brushed

against her leg, for goodness sake, a casual gesture that meant nothing. Thank goodness he couldn't read her thoughts.

She stole a glance at him. His attention was glued on her, not the terrain. She swallowed. His eyes were that warm chocolate color that turned her insides to water. There were gold flecks in his irises, like tiny droplets of sun. She hadn't noticed that before.

His lids lowered as he stared at her mouth. After a beat he raised his gaze and searched her eyes. Whoa, maybe he *could* read her mind.

Pretending thirst, she jerked her attention away and reached for her bottled water. The way things were going, how could she get through the next three hours without making a complete fool of herself?

By keeping her head. Dena compressed her lips and pulled herself together. She wasn't interested in Will, not the least bit.

Right. And the moon is made of Camembert cheese.

"I see something big over there!" Harry exclaimed.

"Me, too!" Chad echoed. "What is it? Can we stop?"

"Hang on." Steve signaled and pulled over. "Where?"

Both boys pointed out the window. "Behind those rocks."

Dena squinted at the terrain and tried to see what had caught the boys' notice. As long as she focused on what was out there and on the kids, she'd be fine. It might take every ounce of willpower she possessed, but she could do that.

* * *

Will forked the last of his deep-dish apple cobbler and popped it into his mouth, chewing with relish. The canyon ride this afternoon hadn't been half-bad, and neither had dinner. He glanced at his son. "Great meal, huh?"

"Mmm-hmm." The boy shoveled another spoonful of a three-scoop hot-fudge sundae into his mouth. He wasn't exactly talking a blue streak the way he did around Chad, but at least he hadn't frowned lately.

Pleased with himself, Will stretched his legs out under the table and laid down his napkin. He'd called the office before dinner. Cal had towed the line on the land deal, and the seller had agreed to most of the terms. The contract and Cal's notes had been overnighted, and Will planned to review them when they arrived in the morning. Which left him the whole evening to spend with Harry and Dena.

And provided another opportunity to show them that he could relax and enjoy himself. And that maybe he'd started to figure out this father thing. Not a bad thought.

Beside him, Dena made a small sound of satisfaction as she finished her butter pecan cake. Did she make similar noises when she made love?

Will pushed his plate and that intriguing image aside. He'd wanted to kiss her since that canyon trip this afternoon. If he were honest, he'd wanted to kiss her from the moment they'd met. Today he'd almost lost his head and done it. Sitting beside her, looking into those big blue eyes, had made her hard to resist.

But he was no fool. He would do nothing to jeopardize her staying. Besides, once he kissed her, he knew he'd want more. He couldn't cross that line, not with Dena. She was Harry's nanny. And Harry came first.

Kissing her was out of the question, he told himself firmly. His eyes strayed to her mouth. The lower lip was plumper than the upper one. He imagined catching it gently between his teeth and nibbling. Then he'd...

"More coffee?" the waiter asked, interrupting the fantasy.

Will started. Just last night he'd sworn to keep those kinds of thoughts out of his head. He damned well better get a grip. If he were smart he'd get away from Dena, leave the table right now. But he didn't.

Dena smiled at the college-age male, making him flush. "I could use a fresh cup."

Red-faced, he complied, then looked nervously at Will. He realized his frown had intimidated the server. Deliberately he lightened his expression and dipped his head toward his white china cup. "Might as well."

Since Harry was still working on that sundae, why not? This was a night to spend with the boy. Will refused to let his lust get in his way. He was a rational and strong man. He'd simply tamp down his feelings and ignore them. He waited until the boy swallowed what was in his mouth, then asked, "What do you want to do tonight, son?"

"They're showing cartoons and a *Star Trek* movie down the hall, for kids only. Chad and some other guys are going." Harry paused, lifted his head and shot Will a cool, defiant gaze. "That's what I want to do."

Will's mouth opened. What the— He'd made himself available, and the kid didn't care. Had this afternoon been some kind of test he'd failed? How the hell was he supposed to know and what should he do now? Unwilling to let Harry see his frustration, he snapped his mouth shut and feigned nonchalance with a shrug. "No problem."

He thought he saw disappointment flash in the boy's eyes, but it was gone before he could be sure.

"Great," Harry said in a toneless voice. He pushed aside his empty bowl and jumped up as if he couldn't wait to get away from the dining room. From Will.

Stung, Will frowned. "That's no way to leave the table, son. What do you say?"

The boy rolled his eyes and released a dramatic sigh. "May I please be excused?"

Will nodded. "That's better. Go on."

"You have fun with your friends, all right?" Dena's tone was light, but a worried pucker marred her brow. "I'll pick you up when it's over."

Will watched his son beat a hasty retreat, weaving between waiters and tables. His shoulders seemed to lift as he moved farther away, as if he'd cast off a heavy burden.

Reaching across the table, Dena touched Will's arm. "Are you all right?"

"Why shouldn't I be?" he muttered. "I've finally decided to spend time with my son, only to find out he doesn't want that at all."

"Give him time, Will." Her eyes radiated sympathy.

He scowled. "I don't need your pity."

"You think I feel sorry for you?" She shook her head. "I don't. You and Harry are going to be just fine. This afternoon proved it. Your being there meant a great deal to him.''

"Did it?" He scoffed. "I don't think he even noticed."

"He noticed, all right. Did you see the way he lit up when the two of you talked?''

Will shook his head. She was trying to make him feel better. Well it wasn't working. "I don't need a pep talk, Dena. I just want to be a good father.''

"I know you do. Be patient. Harry needs time, and he needs to learn how to trust. Today, by coming on the Jeep ride, you took that first step.'' Her gaze met his. "I'm glad you did. And believe me, so is Harry.''

Will couldn't lie to her, not with the conviction shining from those big eyes. "I came with you this afternoon for a reason.'' Her brow furrowed, and he shifted uncomfortably. "I, well, I overheard you and Harry talking in the middle of the night.''

Comprehension dawned on her face. "You mean after the nightmare.''

Her lips pursed and Will braced for a scolding. She must think he was a coward, to eavesdrop instead of trying to help. To his relief, none came.

"I was going to tell you about that later. Since you already know what happened, you understand how important it is to spend time with Harry.'' She folded her hands on the table and leaned forward, her expectant gaze fastened on Will's. "Tell me you'll come to the cookout and rodeo tomorrow. We leave at ten, on horseback.''

Will stared into his near-empty cup. Why should he go? He'd spent an afternoon with Dena and Harry. All he'd gotten in return was a son who preferred the company of his friends to that of his father. Plus a bad case of lust that had pushed his thoughts to where they had no business going and kept his body in a permanent state of semiarousal.

He shook his head. "I expect that contract from Cal first thing in the morning. I'll need to review it and return it with the necessary changes, pronto. That could take a while."

Dena's mouth tightened. "We'll be back by mid-afternoon. Can't it wait until then?"

Will rubbed his chin while he thought about that. He wanted to put that approving light back in her eyes, but he also needed to take care of this deal. "How about a compromise? I'll skip the trail ride, but I'll show up in time to eat."

"How do you plan to do that when the trip takes an hour and a half?"

"They have to get the food there somehow. I'll hitch a lift on the delivery truck."

To his relief, after a moment she nodded. "Fair enough."

In the bar next door, the band tuned up. Dena downed the last of her coffee. "I guess dinner's over." She pushed back her chair and rose. "Good night, Will."

"What's the rush?" He stood up beside her.

Her brow arched in surprise. "I'm in no hurry, but you usually are. You've got a business to run. Don't you have to work on something?"

"You're starting to sound like me." Will chuckled. "Can't do a thing until I get that contract in the morning. Meanwhile I'm a man with time on my hands."

The band struck up a fast country-western song he

recognized from the radio, the kind of music that made a man's foot tap. Without stopping to think, he reached for Dena's arm and guided her forward. "Why don't we go into the bar and dance?"

The large room was smoke filled and loud. Will led her onto a wooden floor crowded with ranch guests and town people looking for an evening of entertainment.

"Come on." He pulled her into his arms. She felt soft and warm and fit perfectly against him. He wanted to pull her closer, but the fast tempo called for less contact and more movement. Grabbing her hand, he twirled her under his arm.

When she faced him again, her eyes twinkled, and a smile hugged her face. "You're good, Will."

It was great to see her happy, even in that ugly dress. "Thanks." He smiled as she copied his step. "You're not bad yourself."

"I took lessons. A birthday gift from my ex-husband."

He swung her again. "Interesting gift."

"He thought I needed to improve my dancing skills." Shadows filled her eyes.

Will wanted to erase them. "I don't know about that, but I think you're great." He grabbed both hands and moved into a jitterbug step. To his relief, her expression quickly lightened.

The song ended too soon. He dropped her hand but they stayed where they were. Though winded and too warm, he was ready to dance the night away. "Want to try that again?"

Dena brushed a strand of hair off her forehead and nodded. "I'd love to."

Breathless and laughing, they stayed on the floor until they were both hot and sweaty and the band called a break.

Will wiped his brow and led Dena to a table. "Let's order a couple of a beers."

He signaled the waitress, then sank into the seat across from Dena's. Her skin was flushed and her eyes sparkled. Hair straggled from her ever-present bun, clinging to her face and neck, and perspiration beaded her brow. She'd never looked more desirable.

He shifted in his seat. The table was so small, their knees touched. He remembered the feel of her bare thigh against his in the van this afternoon. Desire broadsided him. Dammit, he didn't want to feel like this. Shifting again, he made sure not to touch her.

If he were smart he'd leave. Instead, resting his chin on his fist, he studied her. "You're a beautiful woman, Dena."

She shot him a disapproving look. "Tell me, Will, how do you know when someone is beautiful?"

"What?" Will frowned. "I just know, and believe me, you are."

"On the outside, you mean." She shook her head in that schoolish way of hers, and he felt like a kid in a classroom. "That's only window dressing. What's important is what you can't see. I want to be liked for who I am inside, not for what I look like. I don't want to be beautiful."

Will had never met a female who didn't want to be attractive. She was like no other woman he knew. And he still considered her beautiful. This time though, he wisely refrained from saying so. "Another legacy from your ex-husband?"

"He wanted a trophy wife, someone to mold into his dream." Dena's chin lifted defiantly. "That's not me."

"He sounds like a first-class jerk." Will's mouth quirked. "No wonder your marriage didn't work out. You're too bossy to fall into that mode."

"You got that right." She rewarded him with a brilliant smile.

He couldn't help grinning back. Her eyes were the color of sapphires, and right now they were warm and inviting. If he wasn't careful, he could get lost in them. He swallowed and, with effort, tore his gaze away.

The band started up again, this time with a slow song. Will didn't want to dance with Dena. The way he felt, holding her close was too dangerous. He pretended to study the label on his beer.

From out of nowhere, Foreman Bob materialized in front of her. Hatless tonight, he wore a clean plaid shirt and tight black jeans. He nodded at Will then bowed low over Dena. "Hello, little lady. Let's see if you're as good on the dance floor as you are on a horse." He reached out a hand. "May I have this dance?"

Will frowned. "I told you before, her name is Dena. And this dance is mine."

Ignoring her gasp of surprise, he pulled her to her feet.

On the way to the floor, she drew her brows together and shot him a stern look. "What have you got against Bob?"

Will pulled her into his arms. "I don't like the way he looks at you."

She rolled her eyes. "Of course he looks at me. We've been riding together every day. We're friends."

Will searched her face. "That's all?"

"That's all. Listen, I—"

"Good." He settled her firmly against his chest.

She stiffened, but he pretended not to notice. After a moment she relaxed against him. Tightening his arms, he shifted her closer. Ah, much better. He bent down and murmured in her ear. "You smell nice, like fresh flowers and sunshine."

"Thank you, but don't try to change the subject." She pulled back and frowned up at him. "I don't recall anything about dancing in my employment contract. Right now I'm dancing with you. That's because I want to. But later, if I choose to dance with Bob or anyone else, I will."

Will snorted and tried to tug her close again.

Her mouth pursed. "Sometimes you remind me of my ex-husband. He was jealous and possessive."

Well, hell. Will's jaw dropped. "Me, jealous? Ha!" Releasing her, he threw up his hands. "Go ahead, dance with any damn cowboy you want. I won't stop you."

On cue, a tall, good-looking stud, decked out in a fitted shirt and too-tight jeans, swaggered up. Will didn't recognize him as a guest and figured he must live in town.

His gaze traveled slowly over Dena, lingering at her hips and breasts. "Want to dance?"

Will knew she didn't like men looking at her that way. He waited for her to brush off the oversexed jerk.

To his shock she smiled up at the cowboy. "I'd love to." She didn't even glance at Will as she and her new partner whirled off.

They finished the dance and started again. This time, a slow song. Damned if the guy didn't pull her close and kiss her ear. Will's eyes narrowed. Dena pushed away, but the cowboy held her fast.

Of all the— Will's hands fisted at his sides. He didn't stop to think, just strode toward Dena, pushing his way through the crowded floor. Around them, dancers stared wide-eyed. Will didn't care. Gripping the man's shoulder, he jerked him back. "Time's up, bud."

"Okay, man, take it easy." Palms out as a gesture of conciliation, the cowboy backed away.

Dena hugged herself and studied the floor. Tipping up her chin, Will searched her face. "Did he hurt you?"

"No," she said quickly. But the way she bit her lip between her teeth let him know she was rattled.

"Let's get some air." Touching his hand to the small of her back, he guided her through the door leading to the patio and swimming pool outside.

The doors closed and instant quiet settled around them. In the semidarkness lit only by the pool lights, they were alone.

Dena's hands fidgeted at her waist. "I knew better than to dance with that guy. I just did it to prove a point, to show you that I can dance with whomever I choose. Big mistake, huh?" She laughed without humor. "I've never been a very good judge of men." Raising her head, she regarded him with large, solemn eyes. "Sorry I snapped at you."

"Forget it." Will gritted his teeth. "I'd like to smack that bum."

"I'd let you." She offered a wobbly smile.

He grinned back. "Truce?"

"Truce." More hair had worked loose of her bun. She started to fix it, grabbing the clip at the back and pulling the hair tight off her face.

"Don't," he said in a low voice. "Let it down."

She hesitated and he braced for a refusal. Then she tossed her head. Her hair tumbled around her shoulders.

Will reached out and combed it with his fingers. Just as he'd imagined, it was soft as spun silk. Thick tendrils curled over his wrists. "It's beautiful, Dena. You're beautiful." She opened her mouth, but he stopped her with a look. "I know you don't want to be, but you are. Inside and out. I'm not just spouting empty words. I mean it."

Her eyes held his, luminous in the muted light. She swallowed. "Thank you," she finally whispered.

Awareness crackled between them like heat lightning. Suddenly he wanted to kiss her. Had to. Unable to stop himself, he tipped up her chin and caressed her lower lip with his thumb. "Do you know what I want to do right now?"

"What?" she asked, sounding as breathless as when they danced.

"Pull you close and kiss you." He searched her eyes. "But no matter how much I want that, I won't make a move without your okay." Her pupils had darkened, and her lips parted in an unmistakable reply. She desired him, too. His body thrummed. "Tell me what you want, Dena."

"The same thing you do. For you to kiss me, Will." Her eyes fluttered shut as she leaned into him.

He let his mouth brush gently over hers, teasing, until she wove her fingers through his hair and urged him closer. His arms tightened around her as he slowly increased the pressure of his lips.

A sigh escaped from her, and she snuggled against him, her soft breasts pressing intimately against his chest. Groaning his satisfaction, he kissed her again. And again. Impatient to taste her more fully, he angled his head and deepened the kiss, tracing the seam of her lips with his tongue.

She tasted faintly of beer as she opened to him and tangled her tongue with his. Man, she was sweet, sweeter than any of his late-night fantasies. And he was fully aroused. Cupping her hips, he tugged her against his swollen groin. It wasn't enough. He wanted to rip away her dress, feel her naked against him. He wanted to lie down with her and—

A sudden blare of music startled him as the door opened and another couple wandered toward the pool.

What in hell was he doing? He broke the kiss and released her.

"Will?" Looking dazed, she pressed her lips with her fingers—lips swollen from his kisses.

The gesture touched something deep inside of him. Damned if he didn't want to kiss her again. And more.

He wanted an evening of red-hot sex, one passionate night to get her out of his system. Not a good idea, for several reasons. She was his son's nanny. Plus, she wasn't a one-night-stand kind of woman, and he wasn't a long-term-relationship kind of man.

He cleared his throat. "I'm sorry, Dena. I...lost my head."

"I guess I did, too." She refastened her hair with fingers that trembled. "It must be the moonlight and the warm air."

The heat racing through him had nothing to do with their surroundings and everything to do with her. Will swallowed. "Must be."

"I've never...done that before. You know, um, kissed my employer." To his surprise, fear darkened her eyes. "You're not going to fire me now, are you?"

Did she think him that callous? He shook his head. "It was as much my fault as yours. And why would I fire you? You're great with Harry, and he really likes you."

And so do I.

"Good." She bit her lip. "Then can we forget what just happened? I'd hate to think this might ruin the chances of extending my contract."

"Don't worry, it won't," he assured her.

Will knew he wouldn't forget those sizzling kisses, not for a long time. But for Dena's peace of mind he'd pretend. If he didn't, she'd worry about getting fired. Or worse, walk away from him and Harry. He couldn't allow that. Deliberately he changed the subject. "Come on, it's time to pick up Harry."

He was careful not to touch her as they walked back inside. From now on he'd stay away from her. Otherwise he was headed for big trouble.

Chapter Six

A crease marred Harry's brow as he, Dena and Will made their way through the predawn light two mornings later. "It's still dark outside and I'm sleepy," he grumbled. "Why do we have to leave so early?"

Tired and out of sorts from her second sleepless night in as many days, Dena didn't bother to hide her own frown. "I didn't choose the time, the hot-air-balloon people did."

Will shot her a questioning look but remained silent. The darned man appeared alert and rested, despite dragging in late last night. He'd left after dinner, driving to Phoenix to meet with a potential business associate.

Dena hadn't minded that he'd gone, in fact, had been relieved. It meant she could let down her guard and relax, something she hadn't been able to do since those steamy kisses. She touched her mouth dreamily. It had been two days, and she was still reeling. And shocked at her eager response. She'd enjoyed kissing Will far too much. But it had been a mistake, one they both knew was wrong.

He was too much like Reese. Plus, he was her employer. Thank heavens they'd agreed to forget the whole thing, and that he wasn't going to fire her. He'd said he liked how she cared for Harry. Chances were, if she kept on doing well, Will would extend her contract. Oh, how she wanted that. She crossed her fingers.

If she could just keep her head and act like the professional, responsible nanny she was... No problem, except when she was alone with Will. Which she hadn't been, since the other night. He'd shown up at the cookout as promised, and he'd joined her and Harry for dinner last night, but that had been the extent of their dealings with each other.

Even so, the tension that hummed between them was difficult to ignore. Dena didn't like it. And she wished Will hadn't agreed to come along this morning, even if it was best for Harry.

With a warning hiss, the sprinklers on both sides of the walkway spritzed into action, watering the nonindigenous flowers lining the path. Harry squealed as cold water doused his calves.

"Shh," Will cautioned, touching a finger to his lips. "People are sleeping."

Dena couldn't help glancing at him. Why did he have to have those impossibly broad shoulders, and why was his mouth so darned sexy?

He tasted as good as he looked, too. Better. She

stifled a sigh. No man had ever made her feel like that, soft and desirable. In Will's arms her limbs had felt like melted butter. She'd wanted to sink against him and forget about the world....

Annoyed with the direction of her thoughts, she straightened her shoulders. It was time to concentrate on the here and now, on this morning's upcoming adventure. Or misadventure.

She didn't like heights, and she didn't want to be around Will. What in the world had possessed her to sign them up for a hot-air-balloon ride? "This will be loads of fun," she said brightly, partly to reassure herself.

"There's Chad!" His fatigue forgotten, Harry sprinted toward his friend and the rest of the Williams family, who had also signed up for the balloon ride.

Dena watched as the boy dodged a sprinkler without slowing his pace. "I wish I had that much energy," she lamented.

"So do I." Will shook his head admiringly. "If I could package that and sell it, I'd make a bundle."

"Isn't one fortune enough?" she sniped.

Which earned her a surprised look. "What's got you so bent out of shape?"

Contrite, she folded her arms over her waist. "I don't know why I said that. Nerves, I guess. To tell you the truth, I'm not looking forward to this balloon ride. I don't like heights."

"Relax, Dena." Will's mouth quirked in that sexy half smile. "I guarantee you, it's safe."

She wasn't sure anything was safe, not with him standing this close. Even now, knowing how wrong it was, she wanted to kiss him again.

Oh, Lord. Pressing her lips together, she stared straight ahead. In the distance the boys high-fived and laughed. "Look at them. They're growing closer every day. It's a shame they don't live nearer to each other."

"They can still keep in touch. We'll invite Chad to visit this summer," Will said.

Dena nodded. "I'm sure they'd both enjoy that."

She thought ahead to June. Where would she be then? Any day now she expected Will to bring up the future, to ask her to stay on through the rest of the school year, and possibly longer, when they returned to Emerald Valley. She wanted that with all her heart. After all, she adored Harry. He needed her, and so did Will, to help them forge a close and loving relationship.

Plus, with the generous salary Will offered, she'd be able to save some money and start back at the university, taking classes while Harry was in school. Eventually she would earn her psychology degree.

If Will extended her contract. But what if he didn't?

Now there was a scary thought. There were probably other jobs out there, but at the moment she had nothing else lined up. No savings, either, and no place to live. At that daunting thought she hugged her middle.

Will lifted a brow. "Did you say something?"

"No." She managed a smile. Darn it, this was no time to dwell on the negative. She pushed away her fears. She would focus on other, more positive things.

Unbidden she recalled Will's heated expression the other night by the pool. When his eyes lit up with warmth meant just for her, when a genuine smile softened his face, she lost the ability to think clearly. Which was why she'd kissed him.

Partly. The truth was, despite reason and logic, she was in danger of losing her heart. Frowning, she silently berated herself. Will was her employer, for goodness sake, her ticket to job security and financial well-being.

He was Harry's father, a man driven to make money even when he didn't need it. Just like Reese. She couldn't let herself fall for Will. Hadn't she learned her lesson? Down that road lay pain, misery and heartache. She'd had enough of those to last a lifetime. The very fact that she was attracted to Will simply underscored her poor judgment in men.

Tired of her musings, she hurried toward Bonnie and Ted. "Good morning."

The sleepy-looking pair tipped their foam coffee cups in greeting.

At the door to the van a weather-lined, stocky man shook hands with each adult. "I'm Frank, your guide this morning. Climb aboard for a short drive to the takeoff field."

Emmy, Chad and Harry chattered excitedly as they entered the van and found seats. Dena and Bonnie sat together on the bench in front of the children. Will and Ted headed to the back. Over the excited babble of the children, Dena heard snatches of the men's conversation, something about investments and golf.

"Ted and Will get along great," Bonnie said. "Men don't make friends easily. It's nice that they have." Arching a brow, she leaned closer to Dena and lowered her voice. "How are things between you?"

"Harry and Will are doing better," Dena replied in an equally quiet tone. "You saw Will on the cookout yesterday, and he's here today. That's a good sign, and of course I'm pleased about it."

"I wasn't referring to them. What I want to know is, how are *you* and Will?"

Dena leveled a look at her companion. "We've had this discussion before. He's my employer. I'm Harry's nanny. Period."

"Don't give me that." Bonnie shot her a skeptical look. "I saw the way he ogled you when you got on the bus."

Dena's face heated. "You've got a great imagination, Bonnie. Maybe you should take up fiction writing." She quickly changed the subject. "Have you ever been in a hot-air balloon?"

"Ted and I took a ride once, before we were married." Staring at something only she could see, the redhead sighed softly. "We had a wonderful time."

"You weren't scared?"

She grinned and shook her head. "How could I be, with Ted's arms wrapped around me? It was very romantic."

That was the last thing Dena expected or wanted to hear. She swallowed. "I don't think this ride will be like that."

"You never know." Bonnie winked.

Thankfully at that moment, Frank pulled into a large, vacant field not far from one of the horse trails. "We're here, folks. That's my assistant, Jim, waiting for us. He's got everything ready for us."

With the sun hovering on the horizon, the early-morning air was cool. Dena hugged her sweater close and signaled Harry to zip his windbreaker. Ted and Will walked around the huge nylon balloon, which lay spread over the ground, pointing and talking as they rounded it.

Dena, Bonnie and the children watched Frank and Jim tip the huge passenger basket on its side. Then Frank fired up what resembled a blowtorch and roared like a blast furnace. He aimed the noisy machine toward the mouth of the balloon, and the nylon rapidly inflated to a huge orange ball decorated with the ranch logo—black figures of cowboys on bucking horses.

When the balloon was three-quarters filled, Frank lowered the flame, which reduced the noise, and turned to the group. "Okay, folks, listen up. You'll note the basket is divided into three sections." He gestured toward the dividers. "You two," he pointed to Bonnie and Ted, "take the left side. Mr. Williams, you'll climb in first. Once he's in, Mrs. Williams goes. You'll be face-to-face, on your sides, until we right the basket. Careful not to smoosh her, Mr. Williams."

"Smoosh her? Ooo-la-la." Ted widened his eyes and rubbed his hands together comically, and the children giggled. Bonnie grinned.

"Once they're in," Frank continued, "Mr. Stoner and Miss Foster will get in the same way on the right side."

The last thing Dena wanted was to be stuck in a small space with Will. Uncomfortable, she moved toward Harry. "Couldn't Mr. Stoner and his son be together?"

Frank shook his head. "Balance is key here. We need the kids in the middle."

"When do we get in?" Harry asked.

"After the adults are settled, we'll tip the basket upright. I'll get into the middle, and then you kids will use the step holds on the side to climb in with me. Jim and I will help you with that. Understood?" He paused to search all faces, waiting for nods.

"Hold Emmy's hand, will you, boys?" Bonnie asked.

Puffed up with importance, they each took a hand. Eyes huge, the three children stood back and watched.

Frank gave a nod, and Ted and Bonnie climbed into their small partition in the basket, laughing as they adjusted to the space and each other. Within moments they were snuggled together face-to-face, like lovers.

Too soon it was Dena and Will's turn. Filled with misgivings, she watched Will crawl into the small cubicle. Then Frank motioned her forward. Heart thudding, she wriggled into the compartment. In the cramped space she couldn't avoid touching Will. When her thighs brushed his, her face prickled with heat. She jerked back, putting a scant few inches between them. "Sorry," she mumbled.

"No problem." His eyes glinted with amusement. "I had no idea this could be so interesting," he quipped, waggling his brows à la Groucho Marx.

He'd never cracked a joke before. She laughed, and the awkward moment passed.

Frank and Jim righted the basket, and Frank climbed into the center. Per his instructions, Dena and

Bonnie quickly pivoted around, turning their backs to the men.

Frank gestured the children forward. "Okay, kids, climb in the middle with me."

Once Harry, Chad and Emmy were settled, Frank turned up the flame. Within seconds the balloon rose like a billowing orange cloud. The loud hum from the burner drowned out the kids' excited chatter.

Using Will's camera, Jim stepped back to snap a photo of the group. Then he handed the camera back and unhooked the ropes anchoring them to the earth. They lifted slowly off the ground, hovered a few feet above his head and then began a rapid ascent.

Dena glanced down at the treetops below and clenched the rope handles attached to the basket. Fear gripped her, and her heart beat wildly. Why hadn't she waited on the ground, where it was safe?

Too late now.

She glanced at Bonnie and Ted, nestled happily together. Harry, Chad and Emmy wore bright smiles. Dena couldn't even fake a smile. She gritted her teeth against a panicked scream.

"How're you doing?" Will asked, his voice a rumble against her ear.

"I'm a little nervous about this," she admitted.

"Try to relax and enjoy the view. Look, there's the corral. Don't the horses look small? And there's our cabin, with the two purple cacti out front."

His easygoing tone and deep-pitched voice soothed her. She let out a breath and without thinking, sagged against him. His arms circled her. "Look," he pointed over her shoulder, "there's the horse trail you took to the cookout. And that's where we ate lunch."

Keenly aware of the man behind her, she nodded.

"It's nice up here, eh? Peaceful." He chuckled. "Or it would be, if Frank turned off that burner. That thing drowns out everything."

Dena managed a shaky laugh.

"That's more like it." Will's arms tightened around her reassuringly. "Better?"

For some reason, she was. She nodded. "Thanks, Will."

"Anytime," he murmured.

His lips barely brushed the rim of her ear. Dena shivered. At the same time the familiar warmth rushed through her. She knew she should move away, but she didn't.

"Isn't this spectacular?" Bonnie called out, eyeing Dena and Will with interest.

Dena pretended not to notice. They were trapped in this small space, for goodness sake, and she was scared. Will was trying to calm her nerves.

She licked her suddenly dry lips. That explained why her pulse was racing crazily. Didn't it?

"If you look to your right, you'll see a hawk," Frank pointed out.

Dena craned her neck. Behind her, she felt Will follow suit, shifting her against his body as he moved. Her hips naturally settled against his groin.

Dear Lord, he was aroused.

He let out a strangled sound, tensed and dropped his arms. Equally eager to put some space between them, Dena hugged the front of the basket and pretended to focus on the soaring hawk. "Look at him, so proud and free."

Will cleared his throat. "Right now I'd like to be flying up there beside him."

Amen, she added silently. Much as she hated heights, she'd have parachuted out if she could.

For the rest of the trip she held herself stiff. Will did the same, and somehow they managed to avoid physical contact. By the time they started their descent, her muscles ached but her resolve was firmly back in place.

From now on, she'd avoid Will Stoner at all costs.

It wouldn't be easy, but it was the smart thing to do. The only safe thing to do. There were six days left at the dude ranch, six days for Will to watch her and decide whether he wanted her to stay on.

He *had* to want her, had to. For Harry's sake.

She thought about the little boy she'd grown to love, who'd become equally attached to her over the past eight days. The poor child had lost so much in his short life. She refused to add her name to the list. She'd do almost anything to avoid hurting him.

Then she'd best pull her act together. She must push Will from her thoughts and her heart. Professional, responsible and focused. From now on, those words were her mantra. Resolved, she lifted her chin.

"We'll be on the ground soon," Frank warned. "I'll let you know when to assume the landing position."

The balloon swept rapidly over the terrain as they neared the ground. A coyote scurried past, and the children oohed and aahed. Dena smiled at Harry.

"All right, everyone, assume the landing position," Frank ordered.

Shoving her thoughts away, she flexed her knees and braced for the balloon to set down.

Three days later Dena and Bonnie stood arm in arm while Will helped Ted load their rented minivan with suitcases. "I wish you didn't have to leave," Dena said wistfully. "We've had so much fun together."

"I know." Bonnie released a heartfelt sigh. "I feel like we've known each other forever." She glanced at Harry and Chad, who stood talking quietly nearby. "And the boys have become such good friends."

Dena followed her companion's gaze. This afternoon the eight-year-olds' usual exuberance was absent, replaced by somber expressions that made them look older. Even Emmy was sober, hovering nearby as if she understood that they needed time to say their goodbyes alone.

Dena's heart ached for all three of them. Especially Harry. Under Chad's influence he had lightened up considerably from the resentful child burdened with troubles. Who would he pal around with now? "It's a darned shame they have to leave each other," she said.

Ted slammed the hatchback and turned to his wife. "All set," he called as he and Will approached the women.

Bonnie nodded. "Thank goodness for e-mail," she told Dena. "At least the boys can keep in touch."

"I mean it about Chad coming to visit," Will said. "You're all welcome."

"Hmm." The redhead tapped a finger to her lip. "We've always wanted to see the northwest. Maybe we'll take our summer vacation there, with a long stop in Emerald Valley.''

Her husband grinned and dropped his arm around her shoulders. "That's a great idea, honey.''

"Of course it is.'' Her green eyes twinkled. ''Will and Dena can show us the sights.''

Dena felt Will stiffen beside her. He cleared his throat. She didn't wait to hear what he'd say. "Excuse me,'' she said, her face prickling with heat. "I want to get one last photo of the kids together.''

Her well-meaning but pesky friend didn't seem to understand the way things were between Dena and Will. Distant and professional. For the past few days they'd both made sure of that.

If that felt uncomfortable, it was for the best.

For all Dena's efforts Will still hadn't brought up the future. Time was running out, and the uncertainty made her tense and nervous. She only wished she could read the man's mind.

She tugged her bottom lip between her teeth. What if he didn't plan to extend her contract? The thought saddened her, but she'd be hardly surprised, given the way she'd responded to his kisses, the way she still wanted him. He knew it, too, especially after that hot-air-balloon ride. Her behavior on this trip was totally inappropriate for a nanny.

But that was behind her now. Above all, she was Harry's nanny, professional, responsible and focused on him.

And it showed. The boy was starting to blossom. He needed a champion, and she was it. Plus, he was already attached to her. She didn't know how she could leave without causing him serious harm. Not to mention that she needed him. And this job.

Will couldn't let her go, he couldn't! She lifted her head. She would tell him so, too, as soon as possible. This evening she'd promised to accompany Harry to a pool party. Tomorrow night, then, after she tucked him in.

Just in case, though… She'd best phone her boss, Maggie, and ask about other nanny jobs, though that miserable thought knotted her stomach.

Her back was to Will, yet through some kind of built-in radar, she felt his gaze. Refusing to let her worries show, she straightened her shoulders and forced a cheery note to her voice. "Hey, kids, how about a picture of the three of you?" she called out, gesturing them together.

Grins bloomed as they posed like pros.

"That's an adorable shot," Bonnie said. "May we have copies?"

Harry waved his hand in the air, classroom-style. "Me, too?"

Dena laughed. "Tell you what, I'll make one for everybody." She turned to Bonnie and Ted. "How about a picture of Harry and the whole Williams family?"

"Yeah!" Emmy clapped her hands and reached for her parents. "And Dena and Harry's daddy, too."

Dena shook her head. "Someone has to take the pictures. It may as well be me."

"Get over here, Will," Ted prompted.

"Why not?" With a shrug and a grin, Will joined them.

Dena snapped several photos. Along with the other

pictures they'd make a lovely memento of the trip. If things didn't work out, her only memento besides an aching heart.

She gave herself a mental shake. There wasn't one thing wrong with her heart. She was simply nervous about talking to Will tomorrow night.

Surely if she focused the conversation on what was best for Harry, his father would keep her on. Just in case, though, she'd make that call to Maggie.

All too soon she would know where she stood.

The following morning while Dena and Harry lingered over breakfast, Will excused himself and headed back to the cabin. He told them he had work to do, a lengthy real estate document to review and fax back to Cal. Which he did. But there was another reason that pushed him from the table. Dena had asked to talk to him tonight, probably about extending her contract. Will saw no problem with that. He could easily phone Maggie at Nannies R Us and negotiate an extension.

If he decided to keep Dena on. He hadn't made up his mind yet. First, as with any business decision, he wanted to weigh the pros and cons. He didn't need Dena and Harry around distracting him from his analysis.

He chewed on the positives as he strode down the path leading to the cabin. Dena drove him crazy with unasked-for advice about Harry. He frowned. Okay, so that was a negative. On the plus side, there was no doubt in Will's mind that she cared deeply for his son. She'd shown her feelings in countless ways over the past week and a half, both by gifting the boy with much-needed attention and tender affection, and by toeing a firm line when he needed discipline. She knew how to draw him out and how to comfort him in just the right way.

Will shook his head in admiration of her skills. Sure as hell he couldn't do that. Harry appreciated it, too, soaking up her ministrations like a parched plant takes up water. The kid really needed her.

All strong, positive reasons for keeping her with them. So what was stopping him from offering her a contract?

That was a no-brainer. Will glanced down at his groin and snickered. He'd been walking around in a state of semiarousal since she'd entered his life.

He wanted her. In fact, he couldn't remember ever desiring a woman so much. He recalled her eager response to his kisses. She wanted him, too, and that balloon ride several days ago hadn't helped. Sharing a cramped basket with her, feeling her soft body against his, smelling her perfumed hair as escaped strands teased his cheek had nearly killed him. Even now just thinking about her sweet little rear end settled against his groin, heated his blood. He let out a groan.

This constant, pulsing need was a damned distraction, not to mention unhealthy. For that reason he'd avoided being alone with her since the balloon ride, a necessary step to uncloud his mind from the fog she seemed to induce in him.

Could he afford to keep her on, knowing that she had the ability to spike his hormones off the charts? He entered the empty cabin and locked the door behind him, then turned his thoughts to Harry. The boy had seen three other nannies come and go. Will remembered the comment his son had made to Dena after his nightmare, that those nannies didn't like him, and Dena's assurances that she planned on sticking around. What would Harry think if she didn't stay, if Will let her go?

The very thought made his chest hurt. He couldn't do that to Harry, couldn't put his son through the upheaval of yet another change. And he wouldn't.

For the boy's sake it was time to negotiate that new contract through the end of the school year, with another extension if things continued to go well. He'd just have to remember that Dena was off limits, except as a nanny. Now and forever. No problem. He could do that.

He picked up the phone and placed his call to Nannies R Us.

Not long after breakfast Dena stormed into the business center, so mad she slammed the door shut behind her. Will was the only person there, and he looked surprised to see her. "What are you doing here?"

As if he didn't know. She shot him a furious look and marched toward him. "We have to talk."

"Okay." One brow lifted warily as he leaned against the copy machine and eyed her. "Is anything wrong?"

"You bet there is." Halting inches from him, she shoved her shaking hands on her hips. "I just talked to Maggie at Nannies R Us. She says you extended my contract until the end of the school year."

He shrugged. "That's right, at double your current

wages. If things are still going well, we'll extend again.''

Dena brushed off his reply with an impatient gesture. ''Without asking me first?''

He had the gall to look puzzled. ''What's to ask? According to Maggie, you two already talked about it. The deal was, if our two-week trial went well, I'd offer you an extension. I assumed you'd be pleased—''

She cut him off with a rude snort, surprising herself as much as him. But she was too upset to care. He'd done things exactly the way Reese did, with total disregard for her feelings. ''That's just it—you assumed. Before you talked with Maggie about extending my contract, you should have discussed it with *me*. And with Harry. You don't even know whether he wants me to stay.''

''I think it's a safe bet he does.'' Movement flashed outside the open window, accompanied by a rustling noise. Will craned his neck toward it. ''Harry, is that you?''

There was no reply.

Dena glanced around, then shook her head. ''He went down to the corral early, to visit his horse.''

''Are you sure? I swear I saw him out there. This isn't a conversation for his ears.'' Will shaded his eyes and peered through the window.

Dena released an exasperated breath. ''Don't you think I know that? He took an apple from the breakfast fruit basket for Butter. He wanted to feed and brush the horse before the morning trail ride.'' She glanced at her watch. ''I have to head down there soon, so could we please get back to the matter at hand? You assume that if you raise my salary, I'll meekly follow along. Not so.'' Much as she wanted to stay on with them, she crossed her arms and said what had to be said. ''You may be a business dynamo, but you are not a mind reader. What makes you assume I *want* to keep working for you?''

More rustling and rapid footsteps outside the door stopped them both.

Will swore. ''Harry? Son, is that you?''

Worried herself, Dena threw open the door and scanned the grounds. ''There are two little kids playing on the walkway out front. We must have heard them.''

Clearly relieved, Will released a breath. Then he turned back to her. ''I thought you liked my son.''

''Of course I do,'' she snapped. ''I'm crazy about him. But that has nothing to do with this discussion.''

Though Will frowned and crossed his arms, she had his full attention. He was focused solely on her, listening in a way Reese never had, and that felt good. So good that she wouldn't stop until she said it all. ''You rich, powerful men are all alike. You think you can buy and sell people the way you buy and sell commercial property. Well, let me tell you something, Will Stoner. I am not for sale.'' She took advantage of his stunned expression to make one last point, punctuated by jabbing a finger at his chest. ''I'm a human being, and I will not be told where to work. No matter how badly I want to stay or how much money you offer me. If you don't believe me, ask my ex-husband.''

Breathless, she shut her mouth and removed her finger. Or tried to. He grasped her wrist, pinning her hand flat against his chest. His heartbeat was steady, though rapid. Hers was just as rapid. Unwelcome heat climbed up her arm and shot through the rest of her. She twisted away.

She'd just told Will off. Harry's father and her employer, the man she wanted, needed, longed to work for. In an effort to hide the sudden trembling in her limbs, she clasped her hands together and lifted her chin. She could hardly believe her nerve.

Apparently, neither could he. He rolled his eyes. "In other words you want me to ask."

Towering over her, he made a powerful presence in the small space. Refusing to let him intimidate her, Dena swallowed. "That's right."

His jaw set, then he released a frustrated breath. "What kind of game are you playing here? We both know that Harry's been through all kinds of hell the past few months. He needs stability, an adult female he can rely on, no matter what."

"True, but that's not the point, and I'm not playing any games," she began, but Will shot her a quelling look that shut her up.

"That's why Harry and I would like you to come live with us, at double your current salary, through the school year," he said, enunciating each word as if to make certain she understood. "At that time, if things continue to work out well between us, we'll negotiate a longer contract." He paused to look her straight in the eye. "Okay? Is that acceptable to you?"

It definitely was, but the slight lift of his brow made the offer seem condescending. So like Reese. Her temper flared again, but she managed to purse her lips demurely. "I'll have to think it over, and I'm too angry to do that now. Besides, it's almost time for the trail ride. I'd better find Harry."

Will's jaw dropped, and his eyes glittered dangerously, but he managed a sharp nod. Amazed at herself, Dena marched out on legs that shook.

Will replayed what had just happened while he fed his thirty-page document into the antiquated fax machine. Women. He hadn't meant to offend Dena, but clearly he had. He suspected she was a tad oversensitive. That crack about her ex-husband explained why. He must have done a real number on her. Probably tried to buy her affection. A total jerk, that one. Will released a sigh. He should have figured that out. He'd never again make that mistake, never again assume anything about Dena. Despite her anger he thought things had gone well, and he was pleased with himself and fully confident that she would agree to stay on. He'd offered her a generous salary, a luxury home and more time with his son. Things she couldn't refuse.

In no hurry, he stopped at the lodge for a fresh cup of coffee. When he was through, he ambled toward the suite. It was almost time for his daily call to the office. Today he'd remind his brother, Mark, about picking them up at the airport. Once Dena agreed to stay on, he'd also tell his brother that he'd found a permanent nanny for Harry.

Mark liked Harry. Will wondered what his bullheaded brother would think of the opinionated, strong-willed woman he'd hired to care for the boy.

Grinning, he shook his head. *That* ought to be interesting.

The sun beat warmly on his back as he rounded the bend. He almost collided with Dena. "Whoa," he said. "Aren't you supposed to be at the corral? Or were you coming to tell me you're accepting my offer?"

"Thank heavens I found you." Breathless and clearly not listening, she grabbed his arm. "Harry's not at the corral. I can't find him anywhere."

"Relax." Will covered her hand with his and gave a reassuring squeeze. "He has a key, right? He's probably at the cabin waiting for you."

"Right," Dena replied with little conviction.

Side by side, they strode rapidly down the path. Will unlocked the door and Dena shot inside. "Harry?"

Silence greeted them.

"Oh, no." The worry that creased her brow matched the growing unease in Will's gut.

"Maybe he's out by the pool," he said. "You check there, and I'll check out the lodge. We'll meet back here."

"Any sign of him?" Dena asked fifteen minutes later. Her eyes were dark and shadowed.

"Not yet." Will struggled to keep his cool. "Let's check the corral again."

"Good idea. The trail ride starts soon."

But the boy wasn't there. Foreman Bob hadn't seen him, and neither had the other children and adults gathered for the ride.

The cowboy whipped a walkie-talkie from his hip pocket. "I'll contact security."

"Tell them to meet us at the lodge. Come on, Dena." Will reached for her hand. It was ice-cold, as was the fear gripping him.

Where was his son?

Chapter Seven

Huddled on the sofa, Dena sucked in an anxious breath and silently stared at Will's tense back. He'd been on the phone with Sheriff Tate for what seemed like forever, pacing the length of the cabin's living room like a caged lion. As the seconds ticked by, her uneasiness grew. Had the sheriff found Harry? She could discern nothing from the low tone of Will's voice or his rigid posture.

She chewed her lip nervously and waited. *Please.* Guilt and a chilling fear grew within her. Shivering, she hugged her waist. She never should have let Harry out of her sight this morning. If only she'd stuck beside him and waited to confront Will until tonight.

But patience had never been one of her virtues. She'd wanted to talk to him right away, to set him straight and let him know he couldn't get away with making her decisions for her. In her rashness she'd allowed Harry to head off to the corral alone.

Now he was gone.

Kidnapped or worse. Will stretched the phone cord to breaking, as taut as her nerves. Suddenly he pivoted toward her, his face a dark mask. Dena swallowed. Harry could be anywhere, alone and scared or hurt. She shuddered. The last four hours had been hell, the worst of her life. After a hasty meeting with security, the group had split up and anxiously combed the ranch, questioning every person they met. But no one had seen Harry.

Though he hadn't been gone long enough to file a missing person report, they'd contacted the local sheriff, then recombed the corral, the pool area and the game room. Foreman Bob and another cowboy had traversed Harry's favorite horse trails in a frantic search for him. In vain.

Then, having done all they could, Will and Dena had trudged numbly back to the cabin to wait. They were still waiting. If anything had happened to Harry... Unable to sit any longer, Dena jumped up.

Will's back was to her again. Every movement radiated tension. Her hands twisted together at her waist. All his stress and worry were her fault. Misery curled through her, settling heavily in her stomach. She sank back down.

Forget about extending her contract. After this, Will wouldn't want her around. He'd probably fire her the moment this disaster resolved itself.

Dena cringed at the thought. She deserved that and more, and would gladly accept any kind of punishment, if only Harry came back safe and alive. She squeezed her eyes tight and sent up a prayer. *Please, let him be all right.* Then she opened them again.

"Thanks, Sheriff Tate." Will spun toward her as he hung up.

His hair stood up in tufts where he'd run his hands through it, and he looked like he'd aged ten years. But his eyes were free of worry, and the brackets around his mouth had eased. "They found him."

Her frazzled nerves screamed for information as she jumped up and hurried toward him. "And?"

He scrubbed a hand over his face. "He was alone, walking toward the freeway. Except for mild dehydration, he's okay."

"Thank God." Tears of relief filled Dena's eyes. A dozen questions ricocheted through her head, but for now only one thing mattered. Harry was safe and unhurt.

She threw herself into Will's arms. The comfort she found there unleashed the torrent of emotion she'd held carefully in check for hours.

"I was so worried," she sobbed against his chest.

"Yeah, me, too." His arms tightened around her.

"This was all my fault, and I'm s-so sorry."

"Don't blame yourself," Will soothed in a low voice. "It wasn't your doing. We both know that. And, hey, it's over now. Harry's okay. There's no need to cry anymore."

He cupped her head and settled her against his solid chest. Beneath her ear, his heart beat steadily—further reassurance that finally all was well.

No thanks to her. The thought only made her cry harder. "B-but this wouldn't have happened if I'd w-watched Harry. I n-never should have let him out of my sight," she hiccuped. "If anything had happened to him, I'd d-die."

"I know, baby, I know." Will rested his cheek against her head. He was shaking the same as she was, and after a moment, a choked sound escaped from his throat. Dena held him tightly.

Finally he let her go and backed away. His eyes were wet and overbright, his expression raw with emotion. He looked vulnerable and very human.

The sight moved her deeply. Her heart expanded and opened. She didn't want to examine what that meant, only knew she didn't want to leave Harry and Will, no matter how angry Will made her. She wanted to stay with them for as long as they needed her. Even if her heart broke into a million jagged pieces later.

If Will still wanted her.

She pinned her lower lip between her teeth. "Are you all right, Will?"

"Fine." He cleared his throat and rubbed his eyes with the back of his hand. In a blink he shuttered his expression, becoming the cool businessman she knew so well. "Sheriff Tate will be bringing Harry soon. You and I should talk first."

He gestured her to the sofa, then took the wing chair opposite.

Dread filled her. Heaven help her, it was happening. He'd changed his mind. He was about to fire her. Compressing her lips to keep them from trembling, she perched stiffly on the edge of her seat. While losing her job was understandable, she didn't think she could bear to hear the words. Especially from Will.

Tears gathered at the backs of her eyes, but she

blinked them away and lifted her chin. "You don't have to say it. I understand that I've let you and Harry down. I'll pack my bags tonight."

There, she'd done it.

Surprisingly Will shook his head. "You can't do that. We have a binding contract for," he glanced at his watch, "another sixty-four hours. Through the rest of the school year and maybe longer than that, if you decide to stay on."

She couldn't contain her surprise. "After what just happened, you still want to extend my contract? How can you trust me to look after Harry?"

"You care about him," Will said simply. "And we both know how much he needs you."

Little did Will know that she needed the boy, too. She longed to help him and his father continue to forge a good, healthy relationship. But after what had just happened, she wondered whether she was worthy of the task. She dipped her head. "Does he?"

"You're damn straight. Look how far he's come since you showed up. He's happier than I've ever seen him, and I'm very grateful for everything you've done. I want him to grow up in a stable environment, feeling safe and loved. With your help he has a shot at that." His eyes full of feeling, Will sent her a silent plea.

She sniffled and managed a wry smile. "You sure know how to push a person's buttons. No wonder you're so successful in business."

He barely acknowledged the compliment. "Does that mean what I think it does, that you decided to stay on?"

She hesitated briefly, then nodded. "If you're sure you still want me."

"I do. Thank God." He blew out a huge breath, then shot her a heart-melting grin. "You won't be sorry."

"Neither will you," she vowed, silently willing the words to be true. She swallowed.

"But?" The tension was back as he eyed her warily.

Dena bit her lip. The man read her like an open book, and she'd do well to remember that. "I'm sorry I got so angry this morning. It's just, Reese always took me for granted. He made decisions for me without ever considering what I wanted. After the divorce I made up my mind never to let that happen again."

Will visibly relaxed. "I understand." Holding her with an intent look, he leaned forward. "I give you my word that from now on, I won't make assumptions or decisions about your future without asking you first."

"Thank you." Inexplicably her eyes filled.

He shot her a stricken look and quickly handed her a tissue from the box on the table. "Please don't cry again."

"I usually don't act like this, but it's been a very emotional day." Dena blotted her eyes. "When Harry learns that I'm staying, I hope he'll be pleased."

At the mention of his son, Will frowned. "I'm sure he will, but first things first. We'll get to that after we find out why he took off."

"Did Sheriff Tate say anything about that? Why was Harry headed toward the freeway all by himself?"

Will's mouth quirked humorlessly. "He was running away." He squeezed the bridge of his nose as if his head hurt. "Though the devil knows why."

Fresh guilt assaulted Dena. She should have guessed that something was wrong. Though other than missing Chad, Harry hadn't *seemed* upset this morning. "You don't think he was listening in on our conversation this morning?"

Will's jaw set. "I don't know, but I intend to find out."

His face dark, he rose and once again began to pace the room. Dena didn't blame him for being angry and upset. After all, the boy had put them both through hell. Still, he must have a reason for running away. She hoped either she or Will could coax out an explanation. That wouldn't happen if they yelled at him.

"Harry's a child," she said, standing. "Go easy on him."

Will's mouth tightened ominously. "He scared the bejesus out of us. Give me one good reason why I shouldn't read him the riot act."

"Because I should have guessed something was wrong. Heaven knows, I never should have let him out of my sight."

Will frowned. "Quit beating yourself over the head, Dena. The kid's old enough to walk down to the corral by himself."

The words alleviated some of her guilt but did little to diminish her strong feelings about treading carefully with Harry. "He's been through too many tough times. Right now he needs compassion and understanding." At Will's dubious look, she hurried on. "This is a great opportunity for the two of you to open up and really communicate. That way, next time there's a problem, maybe Harry will come to you instead of running away.''

"Don't worry, he'll get a chance to talk." Will crossed his arms over his chest. "And so will I."

Suddenly footsteps sounded outside. *Harry.* Anxious to greet the boy and hold him close, Dena hurried toward the door.

"Wait." Will caught her by the wrist, stopping her. "He's my son, I'll deal with him."

The stubborn set of his jaw brooked no argument. She sighed. "All right. But remember, he's only eight years old."

Will gave a terse nod and strode toward the door.

"If you need help, I'm here," she offered, following close behind.

"Didn't anybody ever teach you to quit while you're ahead?" His eyes narrowed in warning. "Be quiet, Dena."

Nodding mutely, she stood back and mentally crossed her fingers. Don't blow this, Will.

Anxious to deal with his son, Will opened the door and ushered Sheriff Tate out. "Thanks for bringing him home, sheriff."

The hefty lawman tipped his hat. "Glad I could help." He angled his head in Harry's direction. "No more running away, all right, pardner?"

The boy shrugged and stared down at his dusty boots. Dena ruffled his hair, then rested her hands on his shoulders in a gesture of reassurance. His grime-streaked face darkened, then he wriggled out from under her grasp and stared at the Western-landscape painting on the opposite wall.

Will frowned. The kid hadn't said more than a handful of words since Tate had brought him home fifteen minutes earlier, but his hostile expression spoke volumes. He was angry, and closed up worse than Will had ever seen him.

Worry rumbled through his gut. He'd seen this kind of behavior before, years ago, when Mark had had his first brush with the law. Stifling a frustrated sigh, Will rubbed the tight muscles in the back of his neck. He hadn't known what to do then, and he sure as hell didn't know what to do now.

Regardless, he aimed to find out why his son had run off.

The moment Tate's footsteps faded away, he turned his full attention on the boy. "I'll bet you're tired. Sit down, son."

Harry's mouth tightened, but he obeyed. His narrow shoulders stayed ramrod straight, and a small vein stood out on his temple. He reminded Will of a soldier about to head into battle. Putting on a brave front, but scared spitless.

Was that because of what he'd done or because he feared his own father? Doubts assailed Will. He'd planned to bawl Harry out, but maybe that wasn't such a good idea. It sure as hell never had worked with Mark. What *should* he do?

Out of the corner of his eye he glanced at Dena. Her face flashed worry. She opened her mouth, and he knew she wanted to say something to ease Harry's discomfort. Will shot her a warning look. Regardless of his uncertainty this was between him and his son.

She pursed her lips and remained silent. She sat down beside the boy, close enough to reach out to him, but far away enough to give him his space. He wouldn't look at her or Will.

Acting on instinct alone, Will grabbed a chair and slid it across the carpet, facing Harry. "Tell us what you were doing alone on the highway."

The kid stared his hands, locked in his lap. "What do you care?" he finally mumbled.

"No more games, son." Will used the soft, steel-edged tone he reserved for his toughest business negotiations. "I want answers. Where were you going?"

The boy swallowed and paled, but to his credit, he met Will's eye. "To Chad's."

Dena gasped. "But he lives in New York. That's clear across the country!"

Will wondered how the boy had planned to get that far, but set aside the question. There were more important issues on the table. He leaned forward, schooling his expression to idle curiosity. "Why?"

"He's my best friend." Harry shifted, then once again diverted his gaze to his lap. "And his family likes me," he added in a low voice.

"I see." Will grimaced. "And you think I don't."

The kid's half-hearted shrug stung. Will stared at the ceiling and wondered what to do now.

Dena made a small sound that caught his attention. They exchanged a brief look. Clearly she wanted to intervene. Now at last he was ready for her help. He raised a brow, silently acknowledging her. She gave a slight nod and laid her hand on Harry's arm.

"Come on now, sweetie, your dad wants to hear what you've got to say. Give him a chance."

Jerking away from her touch, Harry turned on her, his face contorted with pain and anger. "Why should I listen to *you?* You lied!"

Her eyes widened in shock. "What are you talking about?"

"You said you liked me, but you don't. I listened at the window this morning, and I heard what you told Will. You don't want to stay with us because you don't like me. You're no different from those other nannies."

Anguish filled her expression. "Oh, Harry, you heard it all wrong." She rubbed her forehead as if it ached. "That wasn't what I meant at all..." At the boy's hostile glare, the words trailed off. Her hands fluttered helplessly, then dropped to her lap.

"Dena's telling the truth, son," Will continued, wishing he'd checked the area outside the business center more thoroughly this morning. If he had, he'd have found Harry, and none of this would have happened. "Take it from me, she really cares about you."

"Right." The boy smirked, but Will had his full attention now.

"It's true, Harry," Dena said. "I'm crazy about you. But I was angry at your dad. He made choices for me without asking first. You know how he can be."

Will shot her a warning glance. She ignored it. "Don't you?" she asked, deliberately engaging the boy.

"Yeah, I know," he replied, rolling his eyes.

Dena's shoulders relaxed a fraction. She nodded. "Just like you, that made me mad. So I told him I wouldn't stay unless he asked me. That's the part you overheard. It had nothing to do with you, sweetie." She brushed the hair off his face. "I adore you. You *have* to believe me."

To Will's relief, this time the kid didn't jerk away from her touch. But his scowl was firmly back in place. "Why should I? You're not staying."

"Oh, but I am." She paused to glance at Will. "Your dad asked me nicely, and I gladly accepted. From now until school's out in mid-June, I'm all yours."

Harry looked from one to the other. "Is she telling the truth?"

Will nodded. "She is."

"Oh." The boy picked aimlessly at a thread on his dusty jeans, but his expression brightened visibly.

"That's it?" Will asked. "Just 'oh'?"

One small shoulder shrugged. "I'm glad, I guess."

"That makes two of us." Relief surged through Will. Sliding his chair back, he stood and moved toward his son, clapping a hand on the boy's shoulder. "From now on, if something's bothering you, let's talk about it and see if we can figure out what to do together. No more running away, all right?"

"Okay."

Dena smiled approvingly, and a huge weight lifted from Will's shoulders. He wanted to let out a loud whoop. Instead he nodded soberly. Something important had just happened between him and his son. He wasn't sure exactly what, but he felt as if they'd scaled a rugged mountain together.

Dena stood and offered Harry a hand up. "You really scared me, kiddo. I need a hug."

Opening her arms, she pulled the now contrite boy into a tight embrace.

"I'm sorry, Dena." His voice was muffled against her side.

"I forgive you, sweetie." Her eyes filled as she kissed the top of his head. "And I'm awfully glad you're here with us now."

Will watched the emotional display around a lump in his throat as he awkwardly shifted from one foot to the other. What was he supposed to do now, stand here and watch?

Then Harry reached out to him. Dena shot him a wobbly smile and shifted to make room. The thin little arm held on surprisingly tight. Dena's hip pressed against Will's thigh, and her arm circled his waist.

Her womanly scent of fresh flowers mingled with the odor of sweaty boy. Will's heart pounded and swelled in his chest. This felt good, complete. Like a family. For an instant he imagined Dena as his wife, as Harry's mother.

Whoa, where had *that* come from? One hellish trip to the altar was enough. More than enough. Never again would he get married. He was scaring himself. And he had to get away from Dena, fast. He dropped his arms and quickly backed away.

To his great relief, the first dinner bell chimed. At the same moment Harry's stomach rumbled.

Will glanced at his son. "I'll bet you're starved. I know I am. Let's get cleaned up and eat."

Avoiding Dena's astonished look, he strode rapidly from the room.

* * *

Two mornings later Dena tugged her suitcase into the living room, setting it beside Harry's bags. Down the hall hangers clinked and drawers opened and banged shut as Will packed his belongings. In a few hours they'd leave for the airport and fly to Seattle. From there Will's brother, Mark, was picking them up and driving them the sixty miles north to Emerald Valley.

She and Will had talked last night, ironing out the details, and she knew exactly what would happen then. She'd collect the rest of her things, move into Will and Harry's home and continue as the boy's nanny for three more months, with another option to renew at the end of the school year.

She had what she wanted—a place to live, a generous salary, most days free, and the care of a child she adored. So much to be thankful for, and she was. Really.

Heaving a sigh, she headed into the small kitchen to put away the freshly washed coffeepot and cups. She sponged down the counter one last time. The money Will paid her would fatten up her savings account nicely, allowing her to sign up for more psychology classes at the university in the fall.

She dried her hands on a checkered dish towel and stared out the small kitchen window at the desert scrub and saguaro. Over the past two weeks Will and Harry had made definite progress in their relationship. That thrilled her. It was going to be wonderful to watch as the bond between them continued to deepen and strengthen. To subtly guide them if they needed help.

Yet, pleased as she was for them, she couldn't shake the feeling that things had deteriorated between her and Will. Down the hall a drawer banged shut with loud finality, much the way Will now shut her out. Why? Confused, she turned away from the window and tried for what seemed the dozenth time to answer that question.

Over the past two days he'd changed, starting with that wonderful three-person hug. The first gesture of affection she'd witnessed between father and son, and she'd been privileged to participate in it. Her heart had overflowed to be included in that intimate embrace.

Apparently Will hadn't shared the sentiment. She still remembered the way he'd suddenly released her, his expression at first wary, then shuttered. Since then he'd maintained a cool distance. Other than discussing Harry and the details of her contract, he'd all but ignored her.

He'd forgiven her for the mishap with the boy, and the two males were getting along better. So what had gone wrong? If she didn't know better, she'd think Will disliked her.

She moved hesitantly into the hall. Should she pretend not to notice? Probably. Then again, she wasn't the kind of person who kept her concerns to herself. She'd tried that with Reese, and look where that had landed her. No, if she planned to live with Will and Harry, she must work hard to keep the communication lines open.

For that reason she really needed to talk to Will about this, find out what was wrong. This time, without anger and away from Harry's prying eyes. The boy was down at the corral saying goodbye to his horse. She'd walked him there herself, and knew he'd stay put until they dragged him away.

Resolved, she straightened her shoulders. This was it, the perfect time to talk. Full of purpose she strode to Will's door. On the unmade bed lay an open suitcase, half full of neatly folded clothes. She couldn't see him, but she heard the clink of bottles being packed in the bathroom. She stuck her head through the door. "Will?"

"Yeah?" he called out.

A sudden case of the jitters dried her mouth. She moistened her lips and swallowed. All she wanted was the answer to a simple question: What had caused Will to distance himself from her? She could do this. "Can you come out here, please? I'd like to, um, clear the air."

"What now?"

She could visualize his exasperated look. Then he appeared, shaving kit in hand. He looked tanned and handsome as always, in a navy, short-sleeved shirt and khaki pants. With narrowed eyes he strode toward her, dropping the kit into his suitcase on the way. "So talk."

She almost lost her nerve. Straightening her spine, she tried to school the same cool expression on her own face. "I seem to have done something to upset you."

Will folded his arms over his chest and rocked back on his heels. "Do I look upset?"

At the moment, with his neutral expression, he was the picture of calm. And careful distance. She shook her head. "Not exactly—"

"Good." He flashed a quick smile that didn't quite reach his eyes. "Now if you don't mind, I'd like to finish packing. We have a plane to catch and I want to be on it." He turned away and whistling tunelessly, tugged open a drawer as if she no longer existed.

Dismissed like a servant. So much for talking things out. And for holding on to her temper, which was rapidly and dangerously escalating. Biting back the urge to stomp her foot and let out a frustrated shriek, she glared at him. "As you wish, *Mr. Stoner*. When you're ready to go, I'll be with Harry down by the corral."

"Don't call me that."

Dena widened her eyes. "Why not? It's your name, and I work for you. After the way you've treated me the past few days, I prefer it."

He tossed a pair of socks into the suitcase and scoffed. "I haven't treated you any different from normal."

"If being formal and aloof is normal, then I'll take something else."

An all-too-familiar frown darkened his face as he eyed her. "Look, getting this fatherhood stuff right is hard for me. But I'm trying, and I think I'm doing a damn good job."

"It's true, you've made great progress." She waited for his nod. "But this isn't about you and Harry, it's about you and me."

"You and me," he repeated, angling his head and frowning as if genuinely puzzled.

Which was confusing. Maybe she'd misinterpreted his distance for something else. He *was* juggling several huge commercial projects. What if he was simply distracted because of his work? She'd look selfish and self-centered. Suddenly she felt foolish. If she were smart, she'd end this converstion right now.

"I thought we settled that the other night." He gave her mouth a heated glance, and she could almost feel his lips on hers. "There is no you and me."

Oh, no, he'd completely misunderstood. She kicked herself for kissing him in the first place, even if it had been wonderful. Embarrassed, she scrambled to explain. "But there is, in the working sense." She swallowed and plunged ahead. "Are you having second thoughts about rehiring me?"

"What?" He looked incredulous. "I thought we were past all that. You're exactly the nanny Harry needs. If I didn't think so, I wouldn't have extended your contract."

Relief poured through her. "So there's nothing wrong."

His gaze combed quickly over her, the sudden, heavy-lidded look making her cheeks heat. Then, jerking his gaze to her face as if he'd been caught doing something he shouldn't, he shook his head. "Not a thing."

"Okay, then." Feeling slightly ridiculous and oddly disappointed, she turned toward the door. "I'll just go and find Harry."

So the conversation hadn't turned out exactly as she'd pictured. At least they'd cleared the air. But why couldn't she shake the feeling that something had shifted between her and Will? As she walked toward the corral, the truth smacked her like a slap across the face. Will wasn't the one with the problem. *She* was.

She was falling in love with him.

Definitely unwise, not to mention dangerous. She didn't want to care for Will, and he certainly didn't have those kinds of feeling for her. She laid a warning hand over her foolish heart. Unfortunately, there was no use trying to reason with it. No, she would just have to pretend that she didn't care a bit for Will, that he was her employer and nothing more.

She thought about the way he'd looked at her, his eyes searching and probing as if he read her thoughts, and released a heavy sigh. It wasn't going to be easy hiding anything from that man. She'd need every ounce of strength she possessed, but she would do it, bury her feelings so deep, she'd forget she had them.

She must. Otherwise, she was in for nothing but heartache.

Chapter Eight

A blast of Seattle's wet April air hit Will as he pushed through the baggage claim doors behind Dena and Harry. He hadn't missed the weather. Still, it felt good to be back in the northwest.

"Brrr, it's cold," Dena said, setting down her suitcase to button her coat. "Zip up, Harry."

For once the boy obeyed without protest.

From the shelter of the passenger pickup area, Will peered through the teeming afternoon rain. Dozens of vehicles rolled slowly past, weaving skillfully between the cars that were stopped to pick up travelers. He didn't see the car he was looking for. Sometime later he glanced at his watch and frowned. Where the hell was Mark?

"What does your uncle's car look like?" Dena asked Harry.

"He drives a black Ford Bronco."

"And he's not always reliable," Will muttered. He was tired and cold and anxious to get home. He wanted to introduce Dena to Mrs. Lettie, his part-time housekeeper. Mrs. L. could show her around, while Will headed for the office and away from Dena. *If* Mark made it before the housekeeper left for the day.

Frowning, Will watched a young couple climb into a cab. If his brother didn't show up, they, too, would take a cab the sixty miles to Emerald Valley. He could easily afford the fare. So what was the big deal? That Mark had let him down? Yeah, that was part of it. In all honesty, though, what really had him tied in knots was this attraction thing for Dena. And that he couldn't seem to control it.

He stared stonily at the rain-slick concrete. When she'd faced him this morning, clearly nervous but determined to talk, he'd nearly lost his head and kissed her. Only through sheer strength of will had he resisted her. Now he wanted her more than ever. But dammit, he wasn't going to have her. His hands tightened at his sides. Not ever.

A sudden gust of wind sent a whiff of her perfume his way. Instantly his body tightened.

He stifled a groan. She was killing him, and she didn't even know it. He'd always prided himself on his strength and restraint. But the woman beside him could erode his self-control with a look. Hell, just by being there.

Pretending to search for Mark, Will turned his back to her and moved away. It didn't help. He was as aware of her as if they were joined at the hip. He stared stonily ahead and swore silently.

This was definitely a cold-shower night.

"Do you want to use the rest room?" Dena asked Harry. He shook his head. "Well, I do. I'll be right back."

A few minutes after she disappeared through the entrance, a horn blared, and the Bronco screeched to a halt at the curb. The door flew open, and Mark hopped out.

"Welcome home, big brother." He clapped a hand on Will's shoulder, then turned toward Harry. "Hey, kid, how'd it go? The old man treat you all right?"

"It was cool," Harry gushed. "I rode horses and took a hot-air-balloon ride. And I made a friend named Chad. He's coming to visit this summer. You'll like him, Uncle Mark."

Will grimaced. Harry and Mark had seen each other maybe seven times. Yet the kid had no trouble calling Mark Uncle. Over the past two weeks, Will and his son had made progress in their relationship. When would the boy call him Dad?

It didn't take a rocket scientist to answer that. When and if Will earned the right. Granted, he'd made progress with his son. But he still had a long way to go.

He watched Mark pop open the Bronco's back gate. At thirty years old, the man was just getting his life together. That was Will's fault, for doing a lousy job rearing his kid brother. What made him think he could do it better this time around? Some men weren't cut out to be fathers.

Knowing that didn't change reality. For better or worse, he *was* a father. And by God, he'd be a good one. At least now he had a good nanny to support and help him.

Oblivious of his older brother's thoughts, Mark eyed Will curiously. "So where's this nanny I've been hearing about?"

"Here she comes," Harry said.

Dena's coat swung open as she sighted the car and hurried toward them. Will could almost make out the shape of her legs under her loose denim jeans. Her long, slender legs. He swallowed. For a long moment her gaze linked with his, warm and yet reserved. She's off-limits, he silently reminded himself.

Her attention shifted to Mark. Will tried to see his brother through her eyes. Tall and lanky, dressed in a gray sweatshirt and faded jeans, his face in need of a shave, he was what some called handsome.

"Hello," she said, slightly winded. "I'm Dena. You must be Mark."

"Guilty as charged." With an avid gleam in his eye, he proffered the crooked grin that drew women like magnets and shook her hand. "Pleased to meet you."

Will tensed, waiting for her reaction. To his relief, though her smile was friendly, she didn't swoon the way most females did. "It's nice to meet you at last. Will's told me a great deal about you."

"Is that so?" Mark's mouth hooked in a pained smirk. "I'm sorry to hear that."

Though his brother had stayed out of trouble for nearly a year, the familiar suspicion narrowed Will's eyes. "Got a guilty conscience about something, Mark?"

"No, big brother, I don't." The younger man set

his jaw. "I thought you'd grow a sense of humor once you left the rat race behind and relaxed. Guess I was wrong." He turned toward Dena. "Good luck putting up with Mr. Rigid," he muttered. "I'll get those bags. You hop into the front seat, where it's warm." He opened the door and helped her into the passenger side.

Will scowled as he followed his brother to the open rear gate of the car. "What took so long getting here?"

"So that's what's eating you. I was busy with something and lost track of the time," Mark replied cryptically. He set Dena's suitcases into the back. At Will's dark look, he rolled his eyes. "You worry too much, Will. Believe it or not, I was working." He pushed the bags aside to make room for more. "I put a fence around my property."

"All five acres?" Will asked, piling on his and Harry's bags.

"Yeah." Mark winked at Harry, who watched the two men with interest. "Could have used your help, kid, but while I was breakin' my back, you were lazing around on some horse."

"How come you built a fence?" the boy asked after he and Will were buckled into the back seat. "Are you gonna get a horse?"

"Nah." Mark nosed the car away from the curb and headed for the freeway. "Judy's moving in, and those two dogs of hers need a fenced yard."

"Moving in?" Will echoed, lifting a brow. She was Mark's only serious relationship since his nasty divorce two years earlier. She had a steady job and seemed decent enough. Will liked her. Maybe at last his brother was settling down for good. He grinned. "I'm happy for you," he said, meaning it.

Mark shrugged and grinned back.

"Like Dena's moving in with us?" Harry asked.

Dena's shoulders jerked up straight, and Will choked on a breath. "Um, no," she began.

"No," he stated at the same time.

Will's brother glanced at Dena, then into the rear-view mirror, at him. "Interesting thought, though."

Clearly puzzled, Harry scratched his head, while Mark's shoulders rose and fell in silent laughter.

Will frowned and resisted the urge to shake his brother senseless for voicing aloud what he was trying to suppress inside. He wanted Dena in his bed. Badly.

But just for one night. Then she'd be out of his system for good. He stared out his window, watching the rain-streaked trees and buildings roll past. That wasn't going to happen. He wouldn't let it. She wasn't the type to settle for one night. She'd leave. And God help him, probably tell Maggie at Nannies R Us. Maggie'd read him the riot act, maybe threaten a lawsuit unless he paid for breaching the contract. She'd blackball him from her client list and tell all the other agencies.

Then they'd be right back where they started, worse even, with Harry feeling dumped and Will desperate to find help. He didn't want to go through that again. Uh-uh.

His gaze strayed to the tight little bun secured at Dena's nape. He preferred it down, loose and wavy around her shoulders. He itched to reach out and tug it loose and then run his hands through its soft silken length. His fingers twitched. He curled them into fists and shifted in his seat.

He needed that cold shower *now*.

Better yet, he'd hit his basement gym and work out for a couple of hours first, then finish with that shower. After that, he'd pick up his messages from his home office, then head for the office downtown. After two weeks away, there'd be plenty of paperwork to wade through, and work always took his mind off his problems. And he sure as hell needed a distraction. He glanced down at his groin, which had ached for days. Once he rolled up his sleeves and immersed himself in the business, he'd forget about wanting Dena.

The rest of the time, he would keep tabs on his brother and work on being a halfway decent father. With all that to keep him busy, he wouldn't have a spare minute to fantasize about the woman in the front seat. In no time at all, she'd be out of his thoughts as anything more than Harry's nanny.

The knowledge eased his mind. Crossing his arms, he sank back against the seat and smiled for the first time that day.

Dena drove up the wide, winding driveway of the exclusive school Harry attended. Though she'd dropped him off and picked him up here daily for the past five days, she hadn't yet tired of the setting. She thought she never would. Lush trees and colorful spring flowers gave the rolling hills and expansive grounds an air of peace and beauty.

As always, she parked in front of the ivy-clad brick administration building. Seconds later the massive bells in the adjoining tower began their three o'clock song, the deep, melodic chimes announcing the end of the school day.

In near-perfect synchronization, the front doors of every building burst open and dozens of laughing, chattering grade-school and junior high school kids poured out. They clustered in pairs or small groups, some heading for the yellow buses parked around the corner, others ambling toward the ride pickup area where Dena and the rest of the drivers waited.

She spotted Harry in the distance. As usual he was alone. Head down, shoulders hunched, he hurried across the well-tended grass as if he couldn't wait to leave.

Her heart ached for him. Once school had started again, he'd lapsed back into the alienated, unhappy child she'd met that first day in the airport. She bit her lip and wished she could shelter him from loneliness and pain. But that wasn't possible.

What she could do was offer love and guidance and arms that were always open. She would also become thoroughly involved in his life and continue to push his father to do the same.

Not that Will wasn't involved already—somewhat. He'd managed to make it home for dinner nearly every evening, a definite improvement from before. He even stayed around long enough to help her and Harry clean up the kitchen. But after that, he usually headed for his home office, leaving her and the boy alone.

Since Will left home each morning at the crack of dawn, she and Harry only saw him for an hour in the evening. If she didn't know better, she'd think he was avoiding them both. Then again, why should that surprise her? Will was a workaholic, the kind of man who put business and money ahead of family.

She too had been busy, learning Harry's schedule and getting settled in Will's beautiful home. She felt reasonably comfortable with both now.

But she and Will tiptoed around each other like nervous strangers. Which was uncomfortable, to say the least. She frowned. She wasn't sure how to erase the tension between them, but she had to do something. And soon. Otherwise she was going to go crazy.

But how? The only thing she knew to do was to talk to him, clear the air. She smiled bleakly. Last time she'd tried that, she'd ended up feeling foolish and realizing that she cared for him more than she should. She thought about the night he'd kissed her. Even now she could remember the solid, protective feel of his arms around her and the bone-melting heat that had swept through her.

She caught herself and frowned. She should be glad she hadn't seen much of Will, should take advantage of his absence to get a firm grip on her imprudent heart. But he hadn't so much as smiled at her, though the heated looks he cast her when he thought she wasn't looking let her know he wasn't immune to her. She wasn't immune to him, either. Absently she touched her lips. She could still summon up that hot, tingling feeling... Her heart tattooed rapidly in her chest.

Panic seized her. *Get a grip, Dena!* If she didn't stop those kinds of thoughts right now, she was headed for trouble. Big trouble. She'd best bury her feelings for Will, and do it now. Right now.

A pair of ducks flew overhead, quacking loudly. Dena watched them land and waddle toward a small pond across the grounds. She'd read somewhere that ducks mated for life.

They knew what was important. Well so did she, and if she ever decided to date again, she'd look for a man who took time to enjoy nature, who put his family first. A man the exact opposite of Will Stoner.

Unfortunately her heart had a mind of its own. It liked Will Stoner. Her mouth twisted at her foolishness, her rotten taste in men. Those warm, seductive Arizona nights and the romantic ranch setting hadn't helped, either.

The car ahead of her honked, and Dena started, her face prickling warmly. She shook her head at her foolishness. It wasn't as if the driver could read her thoughts. He wasn't even aware of her. Jumping from his car, he gestured toward a towheaded boy and girl who looked younger than Harry. "Over here, kids," he called.

"Daddy!" the girl squealed, running into his outstretched arms.

Dena watched the scene with envy and sadness. If only Will greeted Harry with such warmth. Things between them were better, but the two males had a long way to go. The plans she'd made for tonight ought to help. She hoped.

Harry was almost at the car now. Shoving her thoughts aside, she waved, smiled warmly and leaned over to open the passenger door. "How was school?"

she asked after the boy tossed his book bag into the back and climbed in.

"Fine," he replied, ducking his head toward his seat belt. He refused to meet her eye.

Despite her efforts to engage him, he rarely uttered more than a word or two about school. Today she was determined to draw him out.

"Hungry?" She handed him a bottle of juice and plastic baggy of peanut-butter-and-raisin crackers.

"Yeah. Thanks." Clearly ravenous, he stuffed a cracker into his mouth and chewed energetically.

Dena bit back a smile. At least his appetite was good. Signaling, she pulled away from the curb. "I talked with Coach Miller today. He said to show up at practice tomorrow. Afterward, you can decide whether you want to join the Little League team."

Harry swallowed a mouthful. "Okay."

"Great." Dena shot him a grin. If nothing else, sports was a great way to meet kids. If Harry joined the team, she'd go to every game and persuade Will to do the same. "I also spoke to Miss Price. Starting next week, I'm going to volunteer in your class from now until the end of school."

Another cracker halfway to his mouth, the boy paused. One brow cocked curiously. "How come?"

"I thought it would be fun, a great way to get involved with your school. I'm going to help with field trips and art projects. You don't mind, do you?"

One shoulder shrugged. "I guess not." He sucked peanut butter off his knuckle.

"Terrific." Dena released a relieved breath. "Miss Price mentioned a science project that's due in a few weeks. What did you choose?"

"Volcanoes."

"That sounds interesting. Do you need to go to the library?"

"Not yet. Zach is going to do it with me. We have to figure out what we're doing first," he said in a nonchalant tone. But anticipation shone in his eyes.

"Zach, eh?" Dena's hopes soared. Maybe the boy had at last made a friend. "That's nice," she replied, careful to keep the excitement from her voice. No sense overreacting to what should have been a normal occurrence. "Why don't you invite him over to work on it?"

"Yeah." Harry nodded thoughtfully and for the first time, looked at her. "Do you think Will would mind?"

"If your friend visited?" Dena flashed him a crooked grin. "Oh, honey, I think your dad would be pleased. You can check with him tonight."

"Okay." Harry frowned and focused on twisting the cap off his drink.

What was it that made his expression darken? She hoped her announcement would change that. "Guess what? Since this is our first Friday night in Emerald Valley, we're celebrating by having your favorite meal."

"Pizza with sausage and mushrooms?" The boy licked his lips and rubbed his stomach.

Dena laughed. "And butterscotch-swirl ice cream with Mrs. L.'s hot-fudge sauce for dessert."

"All right." He flashed her a hundred-watt grin that warmed her heart.

The light ahead turned red. Slowing, she eased into

the left-hand-turn lane. "I thought we'd rent a couple of your favorite movies, too."

"The *Star Wars Trilogy?*"

"Yep. Since it's Friday night, you can stay up late and watch the first two. We'll save the third one for tomorrow." The light turned green. "Mind if we stop at the video store on the way home?"

"Okay," Harry said, with more enthusiasm than he'd shown since Arizona.

Dena gave herself a silent thumbs-up. If things went according to plan, Harry and Will would spend the evening together, just the two of them. She imagined them sharing a big bowl of popcorn in front of the wide-screen TV in the entertainment center off the living room. A great opportunity for the two Stoner males to bond.

She glanced at the suddenly energetic boy squirming with excitement beside her. His well-being meant a great deal to her. She wanted Will and Harry to spend plenty of time together this weekend. Because the key to the boy's happiness lay with his father.

Funny how her own happiness also linked with Will. Harry needed Will's love and attention. And she wanted...never mind that. If Harry were happy, surely the ache in her heart would ease.

That's not the only reason your heart aches and you know it. A heavy sigh escaped from her lips.

Harry jerked his attention her way, his small brow wrinkled. "What's the matter, Dena?"

"Nothing, sweetie." *Except that I'm falling in love with your father.* Forcing a reassuring smile, she turned her thoughts from her worries. "Just tired. It's been a long week. I'm glad the weekend is here."

"Me too."

She turned into the parking lot. She must stay focused on the little boy who depended on her. And help him and his father strengthen their burgeoning relationship.

As Harry's nanny, she owed that to them both. She could do that, work to bring Will and Harry together. Shoulders high, she pulled into a parking space. That was her goal, and all the satisfaction she needed to fill up the emptiness inside. Wasn't it?

Chapter Nine

Will finished his beer, wiped his mouth and eyed the remaining slice of the extra-large pizza he, Harry and Dena had just consumed. "Better finish that, son."

The kid patted his belly and huffed out a contented sigh that Will couldn't help echoing. "I can't. You eat it."

"No way." Stretching his legs under the table, he nudged his chin toward Dena. "How about it?"

"Are you kidding?" Eyes twinkling, she leaned forward on her elbows over her empty plate. "I'm so full, there's no room for dessert."

The easy smile on her face pleased Will. His mouth quirked. "Dessert?"

Harry nodded enthusiastically. "Butterscotch-swirl ice cream with Mrs. L.'s hot-fudge sauce."

Will released a lighthearted groan. "I'll settle for coffee instead." He stacked the plates and started to rise.

"I'll make it," Dena said. Jumping up, she grabbed the dishes from him. "You keep Harry company."

Will exchanged a glance with the boy and shrugged, then let his gaze wander through the bay window. They were sitting in the breakfast room off the kitchen, and the backyard, patio and a large flower garden filled his view. The gardener had planted tulips, daffodils, iris and some kind of flowering bush. All were in full bloom.

He released an appreciative sigh, feeling more relaxed than he had in a long time. Keeping his distance the past week and working out definitely had helped curb his hunger for Dena.

"Tell your dad about Little League," she called from the kitchen.

Suddenly shy, Harry dipped his head and replied softly, "Dena's taking me to practice tomorrow. If I'm good enough, I can join the team."

"Sounds great." Will crossed his arms loosely over his chest. "I always wanted to play sports, but never had the chance."

"Why not?"

"My dad died, and suddenly my mother had to work two full-time jobs. She was too busy to look after us, so I had to stay home and take care of your uncle Mark."

"I didn't know that," Harry said. "How old were you?"

"Eight. Your age." But he'd had to grow up fast. The sympathetic understanding in the boy's eyes caught Will off guard, made his son seem older than his years. "Did you miss him?"

"My dad?" Will cleared his throat. He didn't like to talk about his past, but Harry had the right to know. "A lot. The same way you miss your mom."

"I don't miss her too much," the boy replied stoically. But his expression grew sad and troubled. Blinking, he bit his lip in a valiant struggle not to cry.

Will shifted uncomfortably, wondering how to ease his son's pain. Feeling awkward, he cupped one narrow shoulder and squeezed gently. "Your mom was a good woman. You'll never forget her, and you'll always love her. But after a while when you think about her, it won't hurt so much."

"Really?" Sober brown eyes probed his.

"Really." Something in his expression prompted Will to add, "I only wish she'd told me about you before the accident."

Harry's mouth compressed and he jerked his gaze away, then ducked out of Will's grasp. "She said you didn't want me."

The words were laced with pain. Will winced, both for himself and his son. "That's not true, Harry."

"She wouldn't lie!" Tears filled the boy's eyes, and his face turned beet red.

Will swallowed back his own anger and frustration and forced a reasoning tone. "I don't think she meant to lie, son," he said, "and I'm sure she thought she had good reason for not telling me. Unfortunately, though, neither you nor I will ever know what that is."

The calm tone seemed to help. Harry's flush faded, and he swiped his eyes.

Will continued. "But I swear I never knew about you. Oh, how I wish I had. I missed so much...." He cleared his throat and let the pain, anger and love show in his expression. "You're part of me, my flesh and blood, and I'm so glad you're with me now. I'll always be here for you, Harry. Always." He made a cross over his heart. "That's the God's honest truth."

The boy's head angled as he absorbed the words, and he chewed his lip thoughtfully. After a moment his expression lightened a notch, as if just maybe he believed what Will had said. Will let out a breath and changed the subject. "So, how was school today?"

Clearly relieved to be on safe ground, the boy answered readily. "We have to do a project for science. I picked volcanoes." He slid his glass back and forth across the maple table, leaving a damp trail. "Zach's gonna do it with me."

"He is, huh?" So Harry had a friend. Will masked his pleased surprise with a nod.

"Can we work on it here? Dena said to ask you."

"That's a fine idea."

The boy's mouth curled into a smile. "She said you wouldn't mind."

Settling back in his chair, Will rubbed his chin. Since that miserable episode at the ranch, the kid seemed to be getting along great with Dena. Will knew he'd made the right choice in asking her to stay.

At that moment she appeared in the doorway. She moved carefully toward them, balancing a tray heaped with a steaming coffeepot, two mugs, cream, sugar and spoons.

Will stood and reached for the tray, accidentally brushing her breast. Her startled gaze shot to his as she sucked in a sharp breath. The sudden flare in those big blue eyes reached out, grabbed him and didn't let go.

Familiar heat ricocheted through him, and just like that he was crazy in lust again. *Again?* Still. His blood pounding, he covered her hands with his. "I'll take the tray."

She swallowed audibly. "Thank you." She didn't move and didn't look away. Her lips parted, practically begging his attention.

He wanted to nibble the full lower lip, kiss her until she melted against him and pleaded for more. He could not hide his yearning as he leaned in close. "The pleasure's all mine."

There was no mistaking the hunger in her eyes or the sudden hitch in her breath. She wanted him. His body went on red alert.

"What's wrong with you guys?" Harry asked, and the moment vanished.

"Nothing." Flushing prettily, she shoved the tray toward Will and jerked her hands back. "I'll heat up that hot-fudge sauce and get your dessert, Harry." She pivoted away.

Feeling as though he'd been zapped by lightning, Will set the tray on the table, dropped onto his chair and filled the mugs. What in hell had just happened?

He'd avoided Dena for the past week, as he'd planned. With business booming that had been easy to do. Work had occupied his thoughts and his time, and he'd believed he was past this ridiculous craving for her.

Unfortunately, he'd just discovered that he'd been

lying to himself. He still wanted Dena. More than ever. Groaning inwardly, he frowned into his coffee.

"Here's your sundae, Harry," Dena said as she returned with a bowl. "I hope you've got room for two scoops."

"There's always room for ice cream." He dug in eagerly.

Her smile was wooden as she sat down, grabbed her mug and brought it to her lips. Will followed suit. In the ensuing silence, broken only by the clank of Harry's spoon against his bowl, the tension between them was as thick as the ice cream.

While Harry scraped the last of it from his bowl, Dena glanced at her watch. "It's getting late. If you guys want to watch the first two *Star Wars* movies, you'd better get started."

The boy's small brow furrowed. "Aren't you gonna watch them with us?"

"Um, no." She glanced at him, then at the space above Will's shoulder. "I've got other things to do."

"Oh." Pulling a long face, Harry pushed his spoon across his empty bowl.

Will finished his coffee. If he were smart he'd back Dena's decision. He opened his mouth to do just that, then shut it. His son looked dejected. Not the way Will wanted to end the meal. Couldn't they for once make it through a full evening without a mishap?

He eyed Dena and jerked his chin in Harry's direction. "Come on, for the kid," he cajoled, playing to her weakness for the boy. "It'll be fun."

She bit her lip indecisively and fiddled with her mug, turning it this way and that. "Well, maybe I'll watch the first one."

"Both of them, both of them," Harry chanted, pounding the table in time to his words. Will joined in.

She laughed and threw up her hands in surrender. "Okay, you guys. But it's been a long week. I'm not sure I'll make it through two videos."

The way Will felt, tense and edgy, he didn't know how long he'd last, either. He glanced at his son, who for once in his life looked pleased with himself. The kid wanted them both there. Who was Will to question that? He wanted to talk to Dena, make sure she agreed, but not in front of Harry. He leaned toward the boy. "It'll be late when the movies are over. Why don't you go upstairs and put on your pj's while Dena and I clean up the kitchen."

"I can skip helping you tonight?" At Will's nod, the boy jumped up and shot through the room.

Now for that talk.

Will and Dena cleared the table and carried the dishes into the kitchen. They worked in silence while he put away the milk and sugar and she rinsed the plates and mugs. He couldn't help watching her. A man would have to be blind not to notice the shapely curve of her rear end as she bent over to load the dishwasher.

Then she straightened and grabbed the spoon from the chocolate sauce, first licking it with slow flicks of her tongue, and then popping the spoon into her mouth. "Mmm." She sighed and closed her eyes.

They were the sexiest moves Will had ever seen. Heat thundered through his veins. He stifled a groan.

She was so damned provocative. Only she didn't realize it, which made her all the more seductive.

She pivoted toward him, flushing as she caught him
watching her through hooded eyes. "Oh." Her hands
flew to her chest, chocolate-coated spoon and all.
"You and Harry are doing so well, Will."

"Yeah, we are." He moved toward her. "Tonight's been great so far. We owe you a lot."

"Thank you." She retreated from him, matching
every step and backing up, until the counter stopped
her. "I think." Will braced his hands on either side
of her, and the spoon clattered to the floor. She swallowed visibly. "What are you doing, Will?"

"I want to talk to you about Harry," he said with
the best of intentions. But then his gaze strayed to her
left breast, just above the nipple. "Uh-oh, looks like
you got chocolate on your sweater." The rapid rise
and fall of her chest further stalled his plans to talk.
"We should get that off before it stains." Without
taking his eyes from hers, he sucked his index finger.

She followed his move with wide eyes, flushed
cheeks and parted lips. Will's plans to keep his distance faded in a haze of desire. Blood pounded in his
veins as he rubbed the spot slowly and deliberately,
until her nipple hardened to a tight nub. Dena gasped
and closed her eyes. His body tightened with need.

"This isn't working," he murmured in a hoarse
voice. "The stain's still there."

"I'll put stain remover on it later," she whispered.

"Smart as well as beautiful." His free hand cupped
her other breast, molding its softness in his hand.

"Oh, Will..." She arched toward him.

A growl of approval ripped from his throat as he

palmed both breasts. "I've wanted to touch you all week," he admitted around deep breaths. "That mouth of yours… I really want to kiss you."

"We shouldn't," she said while holding tightly to his middle. She lifted her head. "Should we?" Her tone was full of doubt but her eyes said yes.

"Just once more, to see if it's as good as I remember." He lifted one hand and stroked her lower lip with his thumb. "Then maybe I can get you out of my system."

She searched his face, then let out a sigh. "That sounds reasonable. Unless—"

He covered her mouth with his, before she changed her mind again. Her lips were sweeter than he remembered. With little urging from him, they parted. Her tongue tangled with his as he plumbed the moist, welcome depths of her mouth. "You taste like chocolate," he murmured. "So sweet."

He nudged his thigh between hers, gripped her hips and ground his arousal against her. She made a deep, throaty sound that drove him insane. He slipped his hands under her sweater and up her sleek, hot skin, her bra an unwelcome barrier. He plunged a hand inside the cup, taking her taut nipple between two fingers.

"Don't," she gasped, tearing her lips from his. "Harry will be back soon."

"It'll take him a while. We'll hear him." But Will knew she was right. He also knew they shouldn't be doing this. With regret he released her.

Her breath was as ragged as his as she tugged down her sweater. And that damnable stain was still there, directly over the sharp point of her aroused nipple.

Suppressing a groan, he shoved his hands into his pockets. "I didn't mean for that to happen," he apologized in a low voice. "All I intended was a discussion about Harry."

She lifted her chin. "We're both at fault here." Her hands stole toward her hair, smoothing the strands that clung to her face in tiny, hot wisps. "Well." She tried a smile but it wobbled. "Was it as good as you remembered?"

She nibbled her lip, red and pouty from his kisses, and he nearly lost his train of thought. He jerked his gaze upward. "Oh, yeah."

And as dangerous as a fire in a dry haystack. Bad enough that he wanted her more than he'd ever wanted a woman. But the warmth shining from her eyes was more than desire. Dread settled in Will's stomach. He hoped she wasn't falling for him.

He cleared his throat and backed up, putting a healthy amount of space between them. "I want to explain something to you, Dena. I'm not the kind of man to fall in love. I tried that once."

Confusion clouded her face. "Why are you telling me—"

He held up a hand to silence her. "Turned out, she wanted my money, not me. Certainly not love." He laughed without humor. "When she left, she took my money, the beach house, all the china, crystal, silver and furniture—everything except my business and this house."

"She and Reese would have made a perfect couple," Dena said in a wry tone. "I got my clothes and the possessions I brought into the marriage. He kept everything else. But that was okay. I just wanted out.''

Will nodded. ''Likewise for me. Looks like we both survived. I learned a few things, too. Such as, love is a myth, at least for me.''

''I feel the same way,'' she agreed, meeting his gaze straight-on.

Some of the tension eased from Will's gut. ''Then we understand each other.''

Her gaze dropped to his groin, then lurched up again, and he knew the conversation wasn't over. ''I guess that after tonight, you know I want you. And I think you want me. But making love would be dangerous. I can't promise you more than one night, and you're not that kind of woman.'' He lifted a hopeful eyebrow. ''Unless I'm misreading you—''

''You're not.'' She managed a weak laugh and shook her head. ''I don't have one-night affairs. I don't have affairs at all. Besides, Maggie would fire me in a blink….'' She glanced away and bit her lip. ''Thank you for being honest.''

Despite the desire that still throbbed in him, Will started to feel a whole lot better. He let out a relieved breath. ''Maggie will never know about this. I'm glad we had this talk, Dena, because I can't afford to lose you. Harry needs you too much.''

Was that pain flashing in her eyes? She blinked and it was gone. ''You're right. Harry's needs are what matter.''

Suddenly the boy's footsteps thundered on the stairs. ''I'm ready!'' he shouted.

Will opted to sit alone in the recliner chair and get lost in the movies. He needed to get a grip on himself, tamp down this ridiculous lust that was making him crazy. No matter how much he wanted to make love with Dena, it wasn't going to happen.

He frowned as he absently stared at the television screen, remembering both the haze of desire in her eyes and the matching heat that had raced through his blood. Swearing silently, he scrubbed his hands over his face.

Then again, things could be worse. She could have fallen in love with him. Her bad marriage had taken care of that. Just like him, she was through with love.

Thank God he didn't have to worry about that.

Saturday afternoon Will sat at the large mahogany desk in the home office off his bedroom and stared blankly at the papers he'd brought home. Stoner Enterprises was about to break ground on a shopping complex, and he needed to review the plans one more time. He'd decided to work at home today, and with Dena and Harry at Little League practice and the house quiet, now was the perfect time.

Head propped in his hand, he read the same paragraph for the third time without comprehending a word. He squeezed the bridge of his nose and scowled. Reading this stuff was second nature to him. Why couldn't he concentrate?

Because he wanted Dena. So badly that he'd tossed and turned most of the night. With a groan he shifted his attention to the sliding doors of the office, which he'd opened, and beyond. A soft breeze rustled the trees, and somewhere nearby a dog barked. The flowery scent of spring floated on the balmy air, teasing and tempting.

A beautiful day, and completely at odds with his heavy mood. Shoving his hands into his pockets, he wandered onto the deck off the office. From his second-floor vantage point, he looked out over the backyard, past a stand of fir trees that edged the property, to the dock and lake beyond.

Sailboats dotted the water, drifting lazily. Will thought about the stack on his desk and frowned. He didn't have time for laziness. There was too much to do. Always. No matter how many hours he put in, the workload never lessened. It had been that way since he was a kid, struggling to make it through school, take care of Mark and work.

The memory further darkened his mood. His brother had never fully appreciated the sacrifices, nor had he picked up the same work ethic. He scorned Will for working so hard, accusing him of being too willful and rigid, with no time for fun.

He sure could go for some fun about now, he thought. In bed. With Dena. Those long, slender legs wrapped around his hips as he plunged into her warmth....

He frowned at the stubborn bent of his thoughts. Trouble lay down that road, trouble he didn't want. A kingfisher flew past him, squawking as if to scold, *Then stop thinking about it!* Arms propped on the redwood railing, Will smirked at the bird, whose worries consisted of finding food and helping his mate build a nest.

"Already got my nest, buddy, and I sure as hell don't want a mate." Or a girlfriend or a long-term relationship.

If Dena was sweeter than any woman he'd ever

known, if that soft, yielding body and those generous lips tempted him, and he thought about her as more than Harry's nanny, well... "I'll handle it," he stated to the trees.

After all, he was a man of strength and steely control. Though, God knew, he'd almost forgotten that in the kitchen last night.

Through the window he heard a car and voices. Doors slammed, followed by Harry's rapid chatter, which Will knew meant excitement, and Dena's lighthearted laughter. She laughed like that when she was happy. He pictured her eyes alight with joy, and grinned. The kid must have made the baseball team. Wanting to share in the good news, he headed downstairs.

Dena and his son sat on the brick stoop off the kitchen, drinking pop and sharing a bag of pretzels. The boy wore a green-and-white baseball cap, a matching shirt and baseball knickers with the creases still showing. A brand-new mitt and ball lay on the stoop beside him. He was still babbling with excitement as Will strode toward them.

"—and Coach said we could come to the pizza party after the game next Saturday..." The words trailed off as he spotted Will.

To his chagrin the kid clammed up, as if Will's presence unnerved him. After their great evening together, that stung. How long would it take for his son to relax and trust him?

"Hey, don't stop talking on my account," he said, sitting beside Harry. The bricks were sun warmed beneath him. He glanced at his son, then at Dena on the boy's opposite side. "I want to hear it all. Looks like you made the team."

A beat of silence ticked by. Harry picked up a pebble and studied it. "Yeah," he said, and lobbed the stone into the grass.

Will wanted to bring back his son's exuberance. But how? He glanced over the boy's head at Dena.

"I'm so proud of Harry," she said. One brow arched. "Aren't you, Will?"

"You bet." He clapped a hand on one slender shoulder. "Congratulations, son." He read the logo on Harry's hat. "Lions, eh? That's a good name for a team." When the kid nodded, Will gestured toward the mitt. "That yours?"

"Uh-huh." Harry picked it up and shoved his hand into it, careful to keep hold of the ball. "Coach says to wear it around so I get comfortable with it."

Will rubbed his chin. "Maybe we can toss the ball around before dinner."

Harry finally looked at him. "Really?"

"Sure." Dena's nod of approval shouldn't have made Will feel as good as it did. "When does the season start?"

"We practice every day after school. And guess what?" Harry leaned forward, suddenly eager to talk. "Zach's dad owns the store that sold me my uniform! He's on the team too, so we're gonna car-pool. If I don't miss any practices, I get to play in the game next Saturday. We play the Cubs."

"And I'll be there to cheer you on." Dena's proud smile echoed the boy's. Her eyes sparkled and crin-kled at the corners.

Will liked that sparkle. He grinned.

"You should see your son run," she told Will. Harry's shoulders straightened and his chest puffed out. "He's a natural."

Love shone on her face, and she beamed at Harry as if he were her own child. A boy could hardly ask for more. An odd warmth filled Will, and he silently thanked Maggie at Nannies R Us for sending Dena to them.

Dena glanced at Will. "But, of course, you'll get to see how good Harry is when you come to the game."

Will imagined sitting beside her on the bleachers, cheering for his kid and the Lions. Anticipation brought a quirk to his mouth. Dena would be pleased for them both, which might even keep that enchanting sparkle in her eyes.

He didn't stop to wonder why he found that idea so appealing. "Sounds like a plan."

Midafternoon a week later, Will spun into the parking lot near the baseball diamond. Due to a last-minute meeting with Cal about the new shopping complex, he was late. He glanced at his watch and grimaced. Really late. Worse, the business meeting wasn't over. Will and his attorney planned to reconvene in a few hours.

Surely Harry and Dena would understand, he reasoned as he strode rapidly across the crowded parking lot. He thought about the past week and those nights he and Harry had tossed a ball after dinner. While they played catch, the kid had talked incessantly about baseball practice, the upcoming game and his new friend, Zach.

Will had gladly listened to and encouraged the conversation. For his interest, he was rewarded with his son's growing ease and Dena's pleased approval. That felt good, and all three had looked forward to the game today. Harry had even invited Mark and Judy to come.

Then Cal had phoned about the emergency meeting. Will remembered his son's long face and Dena's disappointment when he'd left this morning, promising to meet them at the game. He frowned. They probably *wouldn't* understand, not any more than they had this morning. Guilt pricked him, but he shoved it away. At least he was here now.

In the distance kids were spread out around the diamond. A small boy swung at a ball and missed. "Striiikkke two," the ump called.

Noise poured from the bleachers and the dugout. Stopping at the edge of the field, Will shaded his eyes against the afternoon sun. The crisp, white numbers on the scoreboard indicated that this was the last inning. The Lions were ahead, five to three.

He scanned the field in a search for Harry, spotting him in the outfield. His attention riveted on the batter, he leaned slightly forward and cupped his mitt. Suddenly he straightened and stared at Will, as if feeling his scrutiny.

For an instant the kid gnawed his lower lip, clearly ambivalent about his father's showing up so late. Hoping to tip the scales in his favor, Will grinned and threw him a thumbs-up sign. Harry didn't return the smile, but his posture straightened. He returned his attention to the batter.

Several teammates stared openly from Will to

Harry. Will pretended not to notice, but he felt like a jerk. A lousy father who'd messed up one more time.

"Strike three!" The ump blew his whistle. "That's three out."

While the teams switched sides, Will headed for the bleachers. Though they were crowded with adults and children, he spotted Dena right away, four rows back, beside Judy and Mark. Heads together, they were talking and laughing.

His hopes lifted. If they were happy, they couldn't be too upset with him. The moment the thought formed, all three turned toward him, and the laughter stopped. They wore dismal expressions, as if he had two heads. Or worse. Just for showing up late.

Fresh guilt assaulted him. He quickly tamped it down. What had they expected him to do, blow off an important meeting? Jaw set, he climbed the risers. Dena's mouth tightened, but it was the disappointment in her eyes that sucker punched him. To add insult to injury, Mark shook his head slowly, his expression full of condemnation. Even Judy, whom Will had met only a handful times, frowned.

Will pretended not to notice. "How much did I miss?"

"Too much, bro." Mark and Judy scooted over, making room for Will beside Dena. Before he even was settled on the hard seat, his brother started in on him. "What's the matter with you, Will? This is Harry's first game. You remember Harry, don't you? He's your son."

"Dammit, Mark—" The people directly in front of them glanced around curiously. With effort Will lowered his voice. "Don't try to tell me what to do when you've never been in my shoes."

Undaunted, the younger brother continued. "That's right, you're the one who always dishes out the unwanted advice. Now you know how it feels." He glanced at Judy. "If I ever neglect a kid of ours the way Will neglects Harry, please take me out back and shoot me."

Were Mark and Judy thinking about marriage? Will was too irritated to care. "The company's about to break ground on that office complex. You know that, Mark. Your future paychecks could depend on it. I didn't plan the meeting. But it's my company, and I had to be there. In fact, I'm heading back to it shortly. I'll explain to Harry and promise to make it up to him next time. He'll understand," he said, with more conviction than he felt.

Mark leaned forward and glanced skeptically at Dena. "Will he?"

"I hope so," she said. But that worried pucker appeared as she looked in Will's direction. "I suppose you're not coming for pizza, either."

Acutely uncomfortable under her scrutiny, he shifted on the hard seat. "You know I want to make it to that party. But I can't, not with this meeting. I'm sorry. I'll make it up to you both."

She didn't even pretend to believe him. Anger flashed in her eyes, but she kept her voice low. "It's Saturday, Will. What's so darned important that it couldn't have waited a few hours?" She shook her head sadly. "But it's not me you need to apologize to. You promised Harry."

Will hated that you-really-blew-it look. He wanted

her to smile, to lose that frosty expression. He also
wanted Mark and Judy off his back. Most of all he
wanted his son's understanding. "As soon as the
game's over, I'll talk to the kid," he vowed. "Hear
that, Mark?"

To Will's chagrin, his brother rolled his eyes.
"The big talk, huh? Whoop-tee-do."

Will ignored the taunt. Dena approved when he
and Harry talked. He glanced at her, waiting for her
nod. She pulled in a deep breath and laid her hand
on his arm. "Things were going so well between you
and Harry. Please, don't go back to that meeting."

Her fingers were warm on his skin. And that
pleading, worried look was hard to ignore. He
thought of the motto on the wall of his office. Do
the Right Thing. He managed that with work, but
what about with Harry? Missing most of the game
and then backing out on the pizza party—it was not
a smart move.

Even Mark was upset. At *Will.* He shook his head.
After years watching his brother on the hot seat, Will
now knew how it felt. He didn't like it. Even if he
did have a valid reason for being late. Mark had
always had explanations for his troubles, but Will
had blown them off as excuses. Now he wasn't so
sure he'd been right.

He rubbed his chin. What the heck, it was his
company. No reason why he couldn't postpone the
rest of the meeting. "All right, I'll phone Cal right
after the game and see what I can do."

"Thank you." The pleased smile that lit Dena's
face dazzled him. Leaning in, she squeezed his arm.
"You won't be sorry."

She smelled of fresh spring air and woman and

promise. Desire slammed through him, along with the urge to put his arm around her and keep her close. But that was dangerous. So he propped his elbows on his knees, stared at the field and ignored the heat pulsing through him.

"All right, bro." Mark sent a teasing look Dena's way, then looked from her to Will curiously. "Say, what's going on between you two?"

Dena flushed scarlet and Will shot his brother a murderous look. "Nothing," he muttered. Just a red-hot fantasy that heated his blood and kept his body on edge for weeks....

"Shh!" Judy elbowed Mark. "Mind your own business."

"Ball one," the ump called, and they all turned toward the game.

"Hey, that's Zach, Harry's friend, at bat." Dena gestured toward the field. "Harry's next up. See him near the dugout?"

Hunching forward, Will watched his son heft the bat on his shoulder and lean slightly in a batter's stance. His tongue poked from the corner of his mouth as he concentrated on swinging the bat. He looked small yet determined and vaguely familiar.

He reminded Will of himself at that age. Willing to give his all, no matter what the odds. Will had always considered having that kind of focus, one of his better qualities. He'd share that thought with his son and compliment him on it.

Amid cheers and excitement Zach scored a base hit. Then it was Harry's turn.

Pride burned in Will's chest as his son stepped up

to the plate. "Knock it out of the park, son!" he shouted.

Dena laughed, cupped her hands around her mouth and yelled, "Get a hit, Harry! Go, Lions!"

"Go, Harry!" Mark and Judy called out in unison.

The boy glanced toward the stands and offered a fleeting smile that faded as he caught sight of Will. Or maybe the kid just wanted to concentrate on the pitch. Will had no time to ponder further. The bat connected to the ball with a loud *thwack*. Harry took off running.

Will jumped to his feet, as did Dena, Mark and Judy. "Run, Harry!" they shouted as the boy rounded first.

An outfielder lobbed the ball toward second base as Zach crossed home plate.

Harry stopped on second. Parents and kids alike cheered. "Way to go, Harry! Great job, Zach!"

Will's son gulped air. Pride showed in his lifted chin and straightened shoulders. Will's own chest expanded. That was his kid down there.

Time flew by, and a short while later the victorious Lions shook hands with the defeated but not daunted Cubs. Spectators stood and headed down the bleachers.

"We're taking off," Mark said when they reached the ground. "We'll congratulate Harry on the way out. See you at the next game, bro—and be on time," he pointedly told Will.

Will definitely did not like being on the receiving end of his brother's advice. But Mark was right. So he forced a nod, then turned away and placed a quick call to Cal. Within minutes the meeting was post-poned half a day, until Sunday morning.

Pleased, he headed toward Dena, and the two ex-cited boys prancing around her. "Mission accom-plished," he announced.

"Wonderful." Her eyes sparkled, and she beamed a million-watt smile just for him. Will felt as if he'd found a cure for cancer. "Let me introduce you to Harry's teammate and friend."

Will shook hands with the boy, then clapped a hand on his son's thin, rigid shoulder. "Great game, guys."

Zach beamed. "Thanks, Mr. Stoner."

But Harry's dirt-streaked face darkened in a scowl as he shrugged away. "How come you were so late?"

Will groaned silently and looked to Dena for help. Her raised brow was like a nudge. "Your dad wants to talk to you about that." Ignoring the boy's stony-eyed frown, she touched Zach's shoulder. "Come on, kiddo, let's ask your parents about carpooling next week." She waved two fingers at Harry. "I'll see you guys back here in a few minutes."

Will watched her go and wanted like hell to call her back. But this was between him and Harry. He rocked back on his heels. "I'm sorry about missing so much of the game. I liked what I saw, though. As Dena says, you're a natural."

"It's no big deal." The boy picked at the lace in his baseball glove.

Will shoved his hands into his pockets. What to do now? He wanted his son to understand. He cleared his throat. "Listen, son, you know I wanted to be here for the whole game. But sometimes un-expected   things happen. When you run your own business, you've got to take care of the problems.''

"Zach's dad runs his own business, but *he* made it to the whole game. He comes to the practices, too.''

"All that, huh?'' Will followed his son's envious glance toward the tall, blond male who was obviously his friend's father. He remembered that the man owned a sporting goods store. He probably had high school kids and other sales staff to help him out. "Well I can't make the practices. But I *can* give you my word about the next game. I'll be there on time.''

"Even if it's in the middle of the week?''

Will might have to juggle a meeting or two, but he intended to keep his word. He nodded.

Harry angled his head and thought about that. "Okay,'' he finally replied, looking both hopeful and doubtful. "Are you coming for pizza?''

"If you still want me there.''

The boy's eyes lit up before he shrugged and ground the toe of his sneaker in the dirt. "I guess.''

Two weeks earlier his seeming lack of interest would have stung. But now Will understood that the boy was protecting himself, kid-style.

So he rubbed his hands together and grinned. "Then let's grab Dena and go celebrate.''

Chapter Ten

Dena's ears rang as she, Will and the other parents followed Harry and his laughing teammates outside. She couldn't help laughing, too. The pizza party had been that good. Raucous and noisy but oh, so wonderful for Harry and Will. Will had made a real effort to be warm and open to his son, and it was working. Tonight the boy seemed to have dismissed his grudge toward his father. Emerging in its wake was a comic, lighthearted side of Harry she'd never seen.

Harry and Will had even played an arcade game together. At last Will's son seemed comfortable with his father. And Will seemed equally at ease with Harry. Feeling somewhat responsible for the small miracle, Dena touched her heart and smiled joyfully. She just hoped their new camaraderie lasted.

Harry and Zach broke away from their teammates

and rushed at her. "Guess what, Dena? Zach and his parents invited me to sleep over!" The boy's exuberance left no doubt in her mind that he was ready for a night away from home. "Can I?"

"May I," Dena automatically corrected. Suddenly nervous, she chewed her lip. While she was happy for the boy, his being away for the night meant that she and Will would be alone in the house. Together. All night. Her pulse skittered wildly at the thought. She was still reeling from that last time they'd been alone in the kitchen—and Will's hands and his mouth and the wonderful things he had done to her. Her traitorous body began to hum and ache for more. Oh, yes, she wanted him. And it scared her.

She swallowed and glanced across a group of parents to where Will and Art and Sheila, Zach's parents, were engaged in conversation. "Better ask your dad." She gestured past a throng of kids and parents. "He's over there."

The boys giggled and zig-zagged through the knot of people, soon reaching their fathers. Dena's gaze collided with Will's. She couldn't read his expression, but she could guess what he was thinking. Because she was thinking it, too.

If they weren't careful, tonight could be dangerous.

Harry and Zach began to high-five various departing teammates while Will and Zach's parents started toward her. She pushed away her unsettling thoughts.

"Think Harry's okay with this sleepover thing?" Will asked. But she knew his question went beyond Harry.

Heat climbed her cheeks. Unnerved by his intent gaze, she looked away. "Fine, I guess."

Unaware of the tension between them, Art and Sheila both smiled. "Great. You can drop him off anytime."

Looking as edgy as Dena felt, Will shoved his hands in his pockets and shifted from foot to foot. "As soon as we pack his bag."

At that moment Harry and Zach rushed toward them, a pair of exuberant, breathless boys. Harry looked up at Will. "Hey, Dad, will you help Zach and me build a volcano next week?"

Pleased surprise flashed across Will's face, and Dena knew that with the use of the word *Dad* the boy had scored a direct hit on his father's heart. Her own heart melted at that. *Way to go, Harry.*

"Sure thing, son." Will tousled Harry's hair with open affection. "Now, let's go home and get your stuff."

Over the boy's head, his gaze hooked with hers. She grinned and gave him a thumbs-up sign to show that she shared his joy over Harry's choice of words. In a blink his expression changed. There was no mistaking the heated look in his eyes. Awareness crackled between them, and Dena's nerves thrummed as if he'd touched her.

Unable to tear her gaze away, she looked her fill while her mind did silent battle with her body. It was a hopeless fight, with her body quickly winning. She averted her eyes, but it was too late. She could no longer fool herself. She was helpless against her desire. She wanted Will to touch her tonight, to make love with her.

But that could cost her this job as well as her relationship with Will. And shatter her heart. Making love would only deepen the emotions she already felt, emotions she had no business feeling. Besides, Will didn't want love. He'd made that perfectly clear. No, she would do the smart thing and resist temptation. The moment Harry left the house, she'd go to her room and stay there until tomorrow morning. That settled, she straightened her shoulders. She could do that. Still...

It was going to be a long night.

Less than an hour later, as Dena slipped into her floor-length terry cloth robe after her shower, she heard Will's Mercedes coupe pull into the garage. He'd returned from dropping off Harry. Despite the fact that she was in her room with the door shut and her resolve firmly in place, her mouth went dry and her pulse kicked up a notch.

She heard the back door open and click shut, and then his footsteps as he made his way down the hall. "Dena?" he called from downstairs. "Where are you?"

Every nerve jumped, and she cursed herself for not leaving a note that she'd gone to bed. What did he want? She opened her door and peeked out. "Up here," she replied.

He took the steps two at a time. "About this volcano thing with Harry and Zach. I—oh." He eyed her with interest. "You changed your clothes."

The heat in his gaze unnerved her, but she managed a casual shrug. "It's been a long day, and I thought I'd relax and curl up with a book," she lied. She'd never been less relaxed in her life. "Could we talk about the volcano project tomorrow?"

"Sure." His gaze dropped to her chest, and she saw with a shock that her collar had somehow veed open. "Sweet heaven, you're naked under there."

Oh, what that low, slightly hoarse voice did to her. Heart racing, she jerked the fabric together. "Oops. I, um, didn't realize..."

Her words vanished as Will's hooded gaze raked over her yellow floor-length terry robe and bare feet. He'd worn that same potent look right before he'd kissed her and done those wonderful things to her the other night. Her traitorous body thrummed. She wanted to fall into his arms, finish what they'd started then....

Flustered, she backed up a step and groped for something to say. "Things went great with Harry tonight, didn't they?"

"Better than I'd hoped," Will said. His eyes fixed on her mouth and darkened as he reduced the distance between them. "But I don't want to talk about Harry right now."

"Oh," she managed. Her heart skittered in her chest, and she couldn't help it, she leaned toward him. "What *do* you want to talk about?" she whispered.

"I don't feel like talking at all. Not verbally, anyway." Heat smoldered in his heavy-lidded eyes. "I want to talk to you with my hands." He stroked her cheek with his thumb. "And my mouth. And then, when you're wet and hungry, I want to join with you."

With every word he spoke, her blood pulsed and warmed and thickened. Until she felt so heavy, she could barely stand. She clutched the doorjamb.

"But I don't want to hurt you," he continued in a

low, sexy voice. "And God knows, I don't want Harry to lose you." That wicked thumb dropped to her mouth and stroked it.

Her lips parted, and she forgot about everything but this moment and loving Will. Consequences be damned. "You won't lose me. I want you to make love with me."

He searched her face. "You're sure?" When she nodded, he widened his stance, slipped his arms around her and eliminated the remaining space between them. Then, finally, he kissed her.

He tasted heavenly, and his arms were strong and *right* around her, as if she'd come home. "Will." She sighed, and for a long, delicious moment, gave in to the familiar, spiraling warmth. Tonight she would love him with her body, she silently pledged, and only with her body.

But her traitorous heart opened and swelled, and suddenly, panic surged through her. She jerked back.

Will wore a confused frown. "Dena. Honey, what is it?"

She struggled to corral her emotions. Anything else was foolhardy and dangerous. She sighed and shifted closer. "Nothing."

Will reclaimed her lips, and her fears faded. Clever fingers molded her hips to his hard groin, weaving magic and heat and want. Then, breathing hard, he broke the kiss. "What I said a few minutes ago about not wanting to talk? If there's something on your mind, better say it now." His penetrating gaze seemed to probe into her very depths. "I don't want any misunderstandings."

"I guess I'm nervous," she admitted.

"Do you want to stop?" He asked gently, while his fingers kneaded the small of her back, sending shock waves up her spine.

Heaven help her, she wanted him to do more of that, on her breasts, between her legs. She pressed closer and shook her head. Right now nothing else mattered but loving Will.

Even as Will deepened the kiss, he knew he should stop and find out what was bothering Dena. But she seemed so eager and willing, and he couldn't get enough of her mouth. Man, she felt so good.

She pressed sweetly against the length of him, as close as possible, given his clothes and her robe. It wasn't close enough. He wanted her naked. He wanted them both that way, with her legs wrapped around his hips while he buried himself in her moist, hot depths. Right here, right now.

He cupped her sexy little rear end and pushed her hard against his throbbing arousal. He was quickly heading to the point of no return. Stifling a groan, he struggled to hold onto his sanity and gripped her hips with shaking hands. "This is your last chance to change your mind. You're sure about this?"

"I wouldn't be here with you now if I weren't." She licked the lips that drove him wild, lips rosy and swollen from his ardent attention.

He imagined her licking a certain swollen part of him the same way. A fresh wave of need exploded inside him. "Are you still nervous?"

"Not anymore," she whispered. She lifted her face and smiled like a woman with a secret. "Now kiss me again."

Then those perfect lips parted, and a haze of desire wiped away his thoughts. He kissed her again, long and deep, showing her his urgent need. The equal fervor with which she returned the kiss excited the hell out of him. With effort he broke it off. "I have protection in my room. Come on."

Dena sagged against him. "To be honest, I don't think I can walk right now."

"I'll get you there." His heart thundering in his chest, he swept her into his arms.

She was quiet, but her hands were busy. She traced his cheek, trailing her fingers down the vee in his shirt in a slow, sensual way that heated his blood to boiling. Impatient but unwilling to take her in the hallway, he gritted his teeth and lengthened his stride, cursing the fact that his room was at the end of the long hall.

He entered through his office and carried her into the bedroom, kicking the door shut behind him. The room was shrouded in the black of a cloudy night. He set Dena on her feet and groped for the bedside lamp. She blinked in the sudden light, her lids heavy and her face and neck flushed with desire. For him.

Will jerked the spread off the bed and tossed it aside. Dena watched him, her hand hovering near her throat as if she didn't know what to do with it. He caught her fingers in his and gently kissed her wrist. "You still okay with this?"

Her pulse fluttered wildly beneath his lips. "Yes."

Holding his gaze, she unfastened her hair and shook it. Blond waves tumbled over her shoulders, stopping on the rise of her breasts, right above where her nipples strained against her robe.

Swallowing, Will lifted a thick, silken lock, letting his hand hesitate over one soft mound. The thin slice of air between his palm and her breast heated, and then he circled the pucker made by her erect nipple. Dena's eyes darkened with need as her chest rose and fell in short, shallow breaths.

"Oh, Will." She reached for her sash. "I want to take off my robe."

"I like the sexy way you say my name." He untied the knot and slipped the terry cloth from her milky-white shoulders. Save for a pair of plain white panties, she was naked. Will smiled. Somehow he'd expected panties like that. Then his smile faded. She had full, round breasts crowned with taut rosy nipples. "You're so beautiful," he whispered.

For once she didn't scorn the compliment, just watched as his hands reached for her. Her eyes fluttered shut as he cupped and kneaded her breasts. "That feels very good," she murmured, arching into his touch.

His own eyes closed as he savored the feel of her hot, satin skin. "I like it, too."

A while later she sighed. "I don't think I can stand up any longer."

"Let's go to bed." He took her hand and led her to his bed, kicking off his shoes and ripping off his shirt on the way.

Dena sank down, and Will quickly joined her. Cupping her shoulders, he guided her back. She settled against his pillow and sighed. With her hair billowed around her like a golden cloud, she looked like a goddess. *His.*

He lay down with her. The feel of her breasts and

stomach against his torso gave him a heady pleasure. His body ached for release, and he'd waited so long for this. But he wouldn't rush. He wanted to make it good for her. So he tamped down his raging need and concentrated on plumbing her mouth with long, deep kisses that made him drunk with the taste of her.

He took his time moving down the graceful column of her neck, stopping to nibble a sensitive place at the crook of her shoulder. Dena moaned impatiently, tangled her fingers in his hair and guided him to her swollen breasts. The blood roared through his veins as he drew one peak into his mouth and swirled his tongue over the sweet, turgid tip.

"Oh," she gasped, arching toward him.

He nipped gently. "Do you like that?"

"Oh, yes." Her fingers locked around his scalp, urging him closer.

Over the years he'd had many women, yet touching Dena felt like the first time. Maybe it was the breathy catch in her voice or the way she responded to him that excited him so. He wanted to make this unforgettable for her.

He moved his attention to the other breast. Hoarse little sounds issued from her throat as she shifted wildly beneath him.

Her response gratified and heated him like a skilled caress. He'd never needed a woman so much. "I want to touch you everywhere," he growled, grasping the elastic waist of her panties. She lifted her hips to help, and then she was naked.

She was perfect, just as he'd known she would be, right down to the thatch of golden curls at the apex of her thighs. Slowly and thoroughly, he explored every peak and valley of her body until she writhed under him.

Finally she stopped him. "I don't want to be the only one naked," she murmured as she unbuckled his belt. "I want to touch you, too."

Will pushed her hands away and quickly disposed of his remaining clothing.

Dena stared at his jutting erection with wide eyes.

His mouth quirked. "See what you do to me?"

"I certainly do." She reached for him, her probing fingers setting him on fire. In a minute he'd explode. He groaned and twisted away. "Let me grab a condom." He jerked open the drawer of the nightstand and quickly sheathed himself, before turning back to her. She opened her arms. He covered her with his body, slipped between her legs, and eased inside. Just as he'd imagined, she was warm and wet and tight. He groaned. "You feel so damn good."

"Oh, Will, so do you." She lifted her hips and wrapped her legs tightly around his hips.

He was in heaven and in hell as he bit back the urge for immediate release. Striving to take it slow, to wait for her, he eased in, pulled out. Again and again the pressure building inside him until he could no longer hold back. As if Dena sensed his need, suddenly her hands clutched wildly at his back. "Harder, Will, oh, please."

He lifted her behind and plunged deeper and faster, again and again, until he was so far inside, he couldn't tell where he stopped and she began.

At last she let out a long mewling sound, gripping his hips with her thighs as she convulsed around him.

The delicious pull of her muscles hurled him over the edge.

"Dena," he called out, and exploded with her in the most intense experience he'd ever had. When he could finally talk, he rolled beside her. "Wow." Threading his fingers beneath her hair, he cupped her neck, massaging her nape gently. "That was incredible."

"It was, wasn't it?" She sighed and leaned into his palm. "It's never been like that for me."

Will felt the same way. He didn't want to examine why. He kissed the tip of her nose. "You're the most passionate woman I've ever known."

"Really?" Her eyes were blue sapphires, and they shone with a warmth and emotion that was easy to read.

She cared for him. A lot. Too much. Uneasy, Will let go of her.

Dena glanced at his face, then compressed her lips, blinked and shuttered her expression. She sat up, tugging the covers with her. "Well," she said brightly. "I think I'll head back to my own bed." The sheet slipped a few inches, revealing the creamy slopes of her breasts. Will's eyes traveled to the twin points, still covered but painfully obvious. Those sweet sensitive nipples he had suckled and caressed until she squirmed.

Desire overpowered him, and his uneasiness faded in a haze of lust. "Stay." He placed her hand on his erection. "I want to make love with you again."

"So soon?" Her voice turned silky as her hand closed sweetly around him.

Half an hour later, spent, he flipped out the light and gathered her close. Her head rested on his shoulder, and her slow, even breathing told him she slept. The musky scent of their joining perfumed the air. Will smiled in the darkness. The second time had been even better than the first. Red hot. Who'd have guessed she would be such a firecracker in bed? Relaxed, satisfied, and bone tired, he pulled up the comforter and closed his eyes.

Dena mumbled, her breath warm and moist on his skin. Desire uncurled in him, stronger than ever. He wouldn't mind waking her up and going for another round. Hell, he wouldn't mind making love all night long. He glanced at the clock. What was left of it. It would soon be dawn.

He thought about opening his eyes in the morning and finding her beside him, a welcoming smile on her face, and her eyes unfocused with sleep. Tenderness he'd never felt before surged through him. He didn't like it. Hell, it scared him.

What was he thinking? That sounded serious, and a serious relationship was the last thing he wanted. No sense taking things further than necessary. Besides, in the morning Harry'd be back. The kid didn't need to know that his father and his nanny were sleeping together.

Make that *had* slept together. Dena was out of his system now; he was sure of it. He frowned at his burgeoning new erection. His body wasn't quite in sync with his thoughts, but by morning it would be. Carefully he untangled his limbs from hers.

She fought separation with throaty sounds of protest as she attempted to snuggle closer. "Don't go. I love you," she murmured.

Love? Will's head snapped up. He'd seen this coming earlier. Why hadn't he followed his instincts and let her go back to her own bed? Any idiot could answer that, even him. He'd been so wrapped up in his damn hunger for her...

He scrubbed a hand over his face and swore silently. A full-fledged headache hammered behind his eyes. He needed space, needed to think what to do. Slipping from his bed, he groped the floor for his shorts, stepped into them and yanked them up.

He was halfway through the door when she stirred. "Will?"

Unready for a showdown, he froze and decided to pretend that he hadn't heard those three dreaded words. "I need to get ready for that meeting with Cal. Go back to sleep."

"At this time of night?" She switched on the lamp, squinting in the sudden light. Her hair was sleep tousled, her lips full and her cheeks rosy. She looked lovely, Will thought with a frown. Like a woman who had just been thoroughly loved.

"You don't have to leave." She tried to reach her robe, but it was too far away. "I'm going back to my own room. Could you hand me my robe?"

"If that's what you want, fine." He didn't try to hide his relief as he scooped the garment from the floor and handed it to her. He turned away as she shrugged into it, retrieving his clothes. He pulled on his jeans and zippered them shut, pretending he hadn't heard what she'd said.

"In case Harry comes home early," he added.

''Really, though, I need to look over some papers before that meeting with Cal.'' He slipped a T-shirt over his head, opened the door to his office and flipped on the light.

By the time he'd sat down at his desk, Dena was at the door. Hand on the knob, she paused. ''Good night, Will.''

''Good night.''

The door closed with a soft click. He closed his eyes in silent relief, then settled down to work.

Dena waited until she was safely in her own bed with the door locked behind her and the covers over her head before she surrendered to the misery wrenching her heart. ''I'm such a fool,'' she lamented, hugging her pillow to muffle the words.

She hadn't meant to tell Will she loved him. But her heart was so full and she was so drowsy and content that the words had just slipped out.

Her confession had upset him. She could tell by the sudden tension in his body, the way he'd quickly moved away from her.

All because she'd whispered the words in her heart.

She closed her eyes around a heavy sigh and let the tears stream down her cheeks. If only she'd stuck to her resolve and kept her door shut tonight. But she'd wanted Will too much for that.

And now...he hadn't lost his heart, but she had.

She was hopelessly, deeply in love with Will. Too bad he didn't want her love. What would happen now? She didn't know, and her cold, lonely bed offered no answers.

She sniffled and blew her nose. There was only one

thing to do to salvage her pride, to fix the mess she'd made of things. People talked in their sleep all the time. She would pretend that she had done exactly that, that she didn't even remember saying, "I love you," and that the words simply weren't true. That one night in Will's bed was enough.

The very idea made her cringe. She'd always prided herself on her honesty, and this lie business didn't sit well. Then again, hadn't she'd been lying about her feelings for weeks now? This was the best, the only solution she could think of. Thank heavens Will only wanted the one night with her. She was strong, she could do this—push her feelings back into hiding, where they belonged.

With an aching heart, she hugged her pillow and tried to fall asleep.

When Dena awoke several hours later, birds were chirping outside her window, and the sunlight streamed through a crack in the curtains. A good omen, she thought as she showered and dressed.

The smell of freshly brewed coffee greeted her as she headed downstairs. Which meant that Will was up. Not that that surprised her. He was an early riser and, besides, he had that meeting with Cal this morning. The thought of facing him made her nervous. Her stomach tensed and she paused on the landing. Maybe she'd stay upstairs until he left. *No.* She straightened her shoulders. She was no coward. She would face Will and assess the damages from last night. She strode barefoot toward the kitchen. Just outside the door she again hesitated.

His back was to her, and she caught her breath at

the sight of him. His hair was wet from the shower and combed back. He wore jeans and a navy T-shirt, the same as that first morning at the dude ranch.

Only a lot had changed since then. She now knew the shape and texture of his body under those clothes, the way he smelled and tasted, and how he liked to be touched. And he knew the same things about her.

But he hadn't lost his heart, and she had. At the moment it was aching wretchedly in her chest. Mustering her courage, she entered the kitchen. "Good morning, Will." She offered a pleasant but not overly warm smile and grabbed a mug from the cabinet, all the while studying him out of the corner of her eye. "You're up early."

"I've got that meeting with Cal." He did not return her smile, in fact, looked pained. There were faint purple shadows under his eyes, underscoring that he'd slept as poorly as she had. He rubbed the red love bite on his neck, then filled her mug, taking care to avoid touching her.

"Thanks," she murmured, lowering her gaze to her coffee.

This was worse than she thought. He could hardly bear to be in the same room with her. That really hurt. Then again, what had she expected? She was the one who had blurted out her feelings.

"It's such a nice day," she said in an effort to break the tense silence between them. "Maybe you and Harry could do something outdoors, like go to the zoo or—"

"Not today. I've got too much work." He shifted uncomfortably, then cleared his throat. "After the meeting I'll be spending the afternoon downtown, at the office.''

"Oh?" Dear God, he could hardly even look at her. She pressed her lips together and gripped her cup, but the question tumbled out, anyway. "This is about last night, isn't it?"

She saw the answer in his eyes. It was. He set down his mug, rubbed a hand over his face and muttered. "We need to clear up a few things..."

It was now or never. Dena lifted her chin and jumped full force into her lie, using the words she'd rehearsed in her head a dozen times. "There's nothing to worry about, Will. I know exactly what happened last night." She offered a bright and hopefully reassuring smile. "And I'm fine with that. Actually, more than fine." In a softer voice she added, "I'm not sorry we made love. I'm glad." That much was true. Except for the damage she'd caused by speaking aloud what was in her heart, she did not regret one incredible moment of last night. She met Will's gaze with a clear, level look, and prayed that he believed her.

"So am I," he said, and for a heartbeat, his eyes warmed and darkened, and her heart fluttered in response. But then, he seemed to catch himself: "Still, I don't think we should have sex again."

"I was thinking the same thing," she fibbed, amazed at her calm nod. At least that way she wouldn't be in a position to let those dangerous words slip out.

"I'm glad we agree," he said. But wariness clung to his expression.

So she quickly segued into the rest of her fabrication. "Did I ever mention that I have this bad habit of talking in my sleep?'' She couldn't meet his eye, so she fiddled with the handle of her mug. ''Mostly nonsense, and of course I never remember a word I've said.''

''Oh?'' Surprise crossed his face.

''All the time.''

Will frowned. ''Exactly how many men have you talked to in your sleep?''

Despite her troubles, she bristled. ''Only my ex-husband. I was referring to girlfriends I used to stay the night with. I was infamous for entertaining them with odd phrases and words.''

''Were you, now?'' The deep brackets around Will's mouth eased.

Dena nodded as relief washed over her. Case closed. Again she smiled. ''Do you have time for breakfast?''

Will glanced at his watch. ''No. I'll be late if I don't leave now.'' He fished the keys from his pocket. ''Cal and I are meeting at a restaurant. I'll grab a bite there.''

''Guess I'll scramble one egg instead of three.'' She hid her disappointment under the guise of topping up her coffee. ''Harry should be home soon. What should I tell him?''

''That I'll see him at dinner and that I'm looking forward to a game of catch afterward.''

Suddenly the phone rang. Will and Dena grabbed for it at the same time. For a moment his hand covered hers. Instant, bone-melting warmth shot through her limbs. Will felt the electricity, too, evidenced by the flare of heat in his eyes. He jerked back as if touching her was the last thing he wanted to do.

She swallowed and answered. "Stoner's residence. Oh hi, Cal. Yes, he's here." She set the phone on the table.

Will waited until she backed away before he took it. "Yeah, Cal." Cupping the receiver between his shoulder and ear, he grabbed a pen and paper from a drawer and began to write. "Got it."

Dena covered her heart with her fist. Apparently, he didn't quite buy her story about talking in her sleep. Well, it was the best she could offer, and she was sticking by it.

She thought about Harry, whose life was finally settling into normalcy and stability. Will had been trying hard, and it was paying off. He'd been nothing but honest with her, too. He was a good man, and she owed him a great deal. She owed it to him to pull herself together and rein in her feelings.

She would do that. Somehow.

If her heart ached, that was a small price to pay.

Chapter Eleven

The air was warm and bright, and the Sunday-morning traffic was unusually light as Will sped down the freeway to meet Cal. These were his favorite driving conditions and just what he needed to relax. He turned up his favorite jazz CD, cracked open the window, shifted into fifth gear and waited for that jubilant, free feeling that came with speeding down an empty piece of road.

It didn't come, nor did the tension in his body ease. His gut felt just as tight as it had in the kitchen, when Dena made that surprising speech.

"I know exactly what happened last night. And I'm fine with that. Actually, more than fine," she'd said. No mention of love at all. He thought about the way her chin jutted forward, and the direct way she met his eye. There was no doubt she meant what she said.

Then she'd surprised him further with that bit about talking in her sleep. He was relieved about that and glad they agreed about no more sex.

So why did he feel so damn confused?

Ahead he saw the exit for the restaurant. As he signaled and slowed to take it, the car phone rang. Thinking it was Cal, he clicked off the CD and punched a button on the speakerphone. "I'm about five minutes away."

"Figured I'd catch you in the car," came Mark's unmistakable baritone. "You headed to that meeting?"

"That's right." Mark rarely hauled himself out of bed before noon on a weekend. Will wondered what he wanted. "What's up?"

"I thought I'd show up and listen in, if you don't mind."

Usually the only thing Will's brother cared about was collecting a paycheck. He frowned. "How much do you need?"

Mark swore. "Why does everything with you have to be about money? I'm interested in this deal and in the company. Is it so strange?"

Yeah, Will thought, but wisely refrained from saying so. "What the hell, why don't you join us?" He gave Mark the address of the restaurant and clicked off the phone.

An hour and a half later Cal left to spend the rest of the day with his family, leaving Will and Mark alone in their corner booth.

Mark waved off the waitress's offer of more coffee, then settled back against his padded bench. "Thanks for letting me sit in. I learned a lot."

"I appreciated your input," Will said, still adjusting to his brother's sudden interest in the company.

"You did? Thanks."

The pleased amazement on Mark's face was out of line with Will's simple compliment. Guilt stabbed him. He didn't praise his kid brother often. Maybe if he had done more of that, Mark would have grown up easier.

"So—" the younger man leaned forward and rested his forearms on the table "—how did that pizza party go?"

Will grinned. "It was wild and loud. Harry had a great time. It's good to see him finally acting like an eight-year-old kid." He couldn't help boasting, "He finally called me 'Dad.'"

"Hey, that's great." Mark gave an approving nod. "You did the right thing, switching the meeting to this morning."

As he had yesterday, Will experienced the odd sensation that somehow the two of them had switched places, that Mark was in the position of doling out the sage advice instead of him. He signaled for the check. "Yeah, well, I sure as hell don't want to mess things up the way I did with you."

"What are you talking about?" The younger man looked puzzled.

"I wasn't exactly the model parent to you. In fact, I screwed up royally."

Mark's eyes widened. "Don't be so tough on yourself, Will. You're only three years older than I. The small age difference didn't exactly qualify you to be a parent. You did the best you could."

"It wasn't good enough." Will laughed harshly.

"That's why you've spent the last fifteen years in and out of trouble."

"Hey, things could have been a whole lot worse. And I'm in decent shape now. I've been straight as an arrow for more than a year."

Will rubbed his chin and considered his brother's words. He'd been so busy with Harry and business that he really hadn't thought much about the changes in Mark.

"So you have." He eyed his brother, wondering where this was leading.

"Know why? Because you never gave up on me. I owe you big for that." Mark swallowed. "That's my clumsy way of saying thank you."

Will didn't have much of a relationship with his brother, and he sure never expected a thank-you. He felt warm and pleased inside, and for a few moments his emotions rendered him speechless. Finally he cleared his throat. "That means a lot," he admitted in a husky voice.

Dena would be thrilled with this unexpected turn in his life, he thought. He imagined her eyes alight with joy and crinkled at the corners from her joyous smile. Then he frowned. Why was he thinking about her right now? He reached for his wallet. "We should go."

"Put your money away. I'll pay."

Will knew he looked surprised. Mark chuckled. "Seeing as I'm feeling generous, and it's a beautiful day, how about I pick up some steaks? Judy and I could stop by tonight for a barbecue at your place."

Old habits died hard. Will narrowed his eyes. "You sure you're not in trouble?"

Mark's hand went up, Boy Scout style. "No more trouble, ever again. I've sown all my wild oats." His eyes twinkling, he gestured Will closer and lowered his voice. "To tell you the truth, I'm thinking about settling down for good."

"No way!" Will laughed. "Are you saying what I think you're saying, that this thing with Judy is permanent?"

His brother nodded. "I love her, Will, and yeah, we've talked marriage. But to tell you the truth, with my track record, I'm a little nervous." He flicked a crumb from the table before fixing Will with a curious look. "So what about this thing between you and Dena? Is it serious?"

It was not a question Will expected, and he wondered what to tell his brother. He pretended to misunderstand. "She's a great nanny, if that's what you mean."

"You expect me to believe that's all she is?" Mark gaped at him as if he had two heads. "I've seen the way you look at each other." He shook his fingers as if to cool them off. "Like there's a fire you can't put out. You sure never had that with Becky."

The passionate Dena was the opposite of his reserved ex-wife, Will silently asknowledged. He thought about last night and the way her body molded perfectly to his, the way her lips parted and her face and breasts flushed with passion that he had incited. His body tightened with sudden hunger. And those sweet little noises she made when he— *No.* He set his jaw. Making love with her was dangerous. Even if she had talked in her sleep, those words had been a warning bell. Thank God they'd agreed to no more sex.

Mark was eyeing him curiously, so he shrugged. "I'm glad you found love, bro, but count me out."

The thought left an empty feeling in his belly. He ignored it. He'd had too much coffee and not enough breakfast. Yeah, that was it.

"That's a crying shame. Seems like you two were made for each other...." At Will's scowl, Mark held up his hands. "Okay, I get the message. Here's my plan—I'm going to pop the question this afternoon. We'll tell Dena and Harry tonight at dinner. Meantime keep the news to yourself, bro. This is a surprise."

Since Will planned to head for the office and stay there until dinner, that wouldn't pose much of a problem. He didn't stop to wonder why he wanted to spend his Sunday afternoon away from home or why he needed to avoid Dena.

But he did, and right now working in his office seemed like his best bet.

Dena finished her steak and wiped her mouth, watching Mark and Judy exchange yet another look only they understood. Throughout dinner they'd acted strangely, lovebirds with a secret. Now it appeared that they were ready to reveal it.

Mark clinked a fork against the cut crystal bowl of his Steuben goblet, catching everyone's attention. "Judy and I want to make a couple of toasts. How about pouring the wine, bro?"

"Me, too?" Harry asked, an impish expression on his face.

"No way," Will replied sternly. But his eyes twinkled as if he too knew their secret.

Mark winked. "There's sparkling cider for you, kid."

"Aw, heck, Uncle Mark." The boy hung his head and pretended to sulk.

Dena caught the grin hovering on his mouth and stifled a smile of her own. Throughout dinner he'd acted happy and carefree, the way a boy should. The tension that had once stretched between him and Will had faded. Just as they had been the night before, they were relaxed around each other, comfortable even. That easy feeling extended between Will and his brother, too. Since yesterday, something had changed between them. It was wonderful and miraculous, and Dena was happy for all of them.

She let out a wistful sigh. If only that camaraderie included her. But the tension had shifted. Now she was the outsider, the one Will was reserved toward. Oh, outwardly he'd been friendly enough, but the cool distance in his eyes had belied his smile.

Dena hated that, wanted things between them to be as they had been before last night, before they'd made love and she'd let those three little words slip out. In order to return to their former, easier relationship, she must convince him that she didn't love him.

Their talk this morning had been a start, but not enough. So tonight she'd worked hard on tamping down her feelings. And done an admirable job, too, she thought, as Will filled her glass. Briefly his eyes met hers. Her heart thudded wildly in her chest. Responding warmth flared in Will's eyes before his gaze shuttered.

Dena stifled a heavy sigh and wondered what she was going to do. She watched Will top off Harry's sparkling cider and take his seat at the head of the table. Mark stood, and she pushed her troubles away. Now was no time to fret. She turned her attention to Will's brother, who tipped his glass toward his nephew.

"My first toast goes to Harry, for that great game yesterday. You played like a team player and a warrior. You made Judy and me proud. Way to go, kid."

"Here-here," Will added.

Glasses clinked and everyone sipped while Harry's small chest puffed out with pride. He quickly drained his glass, then held it out for more. As Will refilled it, the small face lifted toward Mark expectantly. "What's the second toast?"

"I'm getting to that." This time Will's brother tipped his goblet toward Judy. "To the love of my life." He smiled tenderly. "Glad I met you, babe."

The radiant woman flushed with pleasure, then lifted her glass in silent salute. "Thank you, sweetheart."

For an instant their gazes locked. The understanding and love that flowed between them filled Dena with heartfelt longing. How lucky they were to have found each other, to have found love and be glad of it.

Judy turned in her chair to face Will. "And thank you, Will, for raising Mark to be a good man, and for never giving up on him."

Dena watched a slow flush climb up Will's neck and face as he dipped his head. He wasn't good at accepting compliments. "You're welcome."

Mark turned to Dena. "I told him the same thing this morning. Maybe hearing it from Judy will convince him."

Will's mouth quirked as he eyed Mark. "I guess you turned out all right."

The younger man grinned. "If I hadn't, Judy and I wouldn't be getting married."

"She said yes?" Beaming, Will clapped his brother on the shoulder. "Way to go." He leaned over and planted a kiss on his future sister-in-law's cheek. "Welcome to the family, Judy. I'm glad my brother found you."

"Me, too." Mark lifted his glass again. "I want you all to hear my solemn promise—this marriage will last a lifetime and then some."

Dena knew with certainty that it would. Anyone with eyes could see that Mark and Judy were crazy about each other. Envy weighed like a heavy stone on her chest. She would never know what it felt like to share that kind of love. What was that old song about unrequited love? Something about being a bore. Well it was worse than that. It was the pits.

Nevertheless she smiled and hugged the lucky couple, genuinely happy for them. "Congratulations! Can I do anything to help?"

"Boy, can you," Judy and Mark replied in unison. Everyone laughed.

"Seeing how the joyous event will take place in three weeks," Mark explained.

"In our backyard," Judy added. "It won't be a lavish affair, but we want all our friends and family there."

Arm firmly around his fiancée, Mark turned toward

Will and cleared his throat. "I'd like you to be my best man."

The mixture of emotions crossing Will's face showed how touched he was. "It'd be an honor."

Dena's heart expanded for Will and his brother. How wonderful for them to have at last made peace.

"Thanks." Mark nodded once. "Maybe someday I'll return the favor."

Will coughed. "Not likely."

"He's never getting married," Harry explained, clearly parroting his father's words. By the wistful look on his young face, he did not approve of the decision.

"You never know, your old man may change his mind." Mark winked at his bride-to-be. "I did." He glanced slyly from Will to Dena. "All it takes is the right woman."

The boy's wishful gaze followed his uncle's. Dena's eyes widened as comprehension dawned like the morning sun. He wanted Will to marry *her*.

Now there was a ridiculous fantasy—that he would ever propose. Her face heated. She lowered her lashes then glanced at Will, but he was busy refilling the glasses. She couldn't read his expression. He didn't seem to have heard his brother. Or maybe he'd decided to ignore the words.

Cupping the stem of her goblet, she stared into the opaque burgundy liquid. Will wasn't the only one who didn't want to trade wedding vows. She certainly didn't want to walk down that rocky path again.

Not even with Will Stoner. Besides all the obvious reasons—her bad marriage, her desire to earn her college degree and take care of herself—Will didn't love her. She took a fortifying sip of wine.

She thought she'd explained her views to Harry, that night in Arizona when he'd had nightmares. He seemed to have forgotten. Hopefully he'd soon shelve the far-fetched fantasy of his nanny and father together.

"Dena?" Judy touched Dena's arm. "I'd like to ask you something. My sister is my only family. She's an ordained minister, and we've asked her to marry us. I know you and I don't know each other very well yet, but I'm hoping... Will you be my maid of honor?"

"Me?" Delighted, Dena grinned. "I'd love to." She thought about her old, out-of-date clothing. She'd take some of the money she'd saved up for college and go shopping. "What should I wear?"

"Something dressy." Judy propped her chin in hand and eyed her. "With your fair skin and blond hair, you'll look great in my colors, lilac and rose. If you want, I'll get my dressmaker to sew you a dress. She does a great job and doesn't charge too much."

"That would be great," Dena said, "but we'll have to do it this coming week. Next weekend is Harry's carnival, and I'll be busy with that."

Harry scratched his head. "What about me? Am I gonna be in the wedding?"

Mark grinned. "We'd never forget you, kid. You get to be the ring bearer. That's a very important job."

The boy beamed. "Cool."

Chapter Twelve

"So, Harry, what do you want to do first?" Dena asked the following Saturday afternoon as they strolled from a parking lot toward the boy's school. Only it no longer looked like a school. Tents, booths, rides and milling crowds had turned the rolling hills and genteel surroundings into a bona fide carnival.

The mouthwatering smell of hot, buttered popcorn permeated the air, and the boy licked his lips. "Buy some popcorn."

Will chuckled and pulled out his wallet. After the long, tense week she and Will had spent, it was good to hear that warm, spontaneous sound. She laughed, too.

She hadn't seen much of him lately. With his new office complex in its beginning construction phase, he was putting in long, grueling hours. He'd managed to make it home for dinner most evenings, but he often headed back to the office soon after the meal.

It was his company, and she knew there was plenty to do. Still, she had the distinct feeling that her late-night confession had the man running scared. For the hundredth time she cursed herself for letting those three words slip out.

Mentally squaring her shoulders, she renewed her determination to ease the tension between them. Today, their first afternoon together since Mark and Judy had announced their engagement last week, was a good place to do so.

Dena wasn't used to hiding her feelings. Acting as if she didn't love Will was turning out to be more difficult than she'd imagined. But so far today she'd managed well, she thought. Until she glanced at his face.

With Harry gone to get popcorn, Will's jovial mood had vanished. Tension radiated from him, evident in the stiff line of his shoulders and the way his eyes darted over the grounds, lighting on anything and everything except her. Clearly he was still as uncomfortable around her as before. Darn it.

Stifling a frustrated sigh, she forced her attention to the activites around her. The carnival was in full swing. People she recognized from Little League and other school-related events wandered from booth to booth, playing games, munching hot dogs and snacks, and trying out various rides. What to do now?

If she ignored the tension, pretended that things were fine, maybe they would be. At least that way she could make it through the rest of the day without a headache and a bad case of jangled nerves. Deliberately she brightened her expression and her tone. "What do you want to do this afternoon, Will?"

He shrugged. "This is Harry's carnival. Whatever he decides."

Lately their only topic of conversation was Harry. Which was fine with Dena. Parenting the boy was a task they both shared. That was safe ground, and there was always plenty to talk about. She eagerly latched on to the topic. "Since he loves throwing a ball, I'll bet he'll want to try the Ping-Pong toss first."

"Good suggestion. We'll ask him when he comes back."

The conversation stalled. As the uncomfortable minutes ticked by, they both turned toward to the popcorn booth, where Zach and a group of boys from Little League were grouped around Harry.

He said something and the boys laughed. Dena smiled. "Looks like he's found some of his friends. Isn't it amazing how he's changed over the past few weeks?"

Will nodded. "Sure is." For the first time in what felt like ages, he looked at her with appreciation rather than apprehension. "A large part of that change comes from your efforts. I don't know how you did it, but my son has turned into a normal kid."

Both Will's smile and words pleased her. She dipped her head and shrugged. "You're the one who should get the credit. You've been doing a great job parenting."

"With a big push from you. Thanks." His eyes sought hers, and suddenly his gaze lit and heated and things felt normal again.

"Glad to help." She wanted to melt. She missed this, the familiar, aching warmth between them.

Suddenly Will seemed to catch himself. He frowned and jerked his attention to some point behind her. "Here comes Harry."

His friends were with him, talking and laughing. Dena and Will exchanged greetings with them and accepted tastes of popcorn. His mouth full, Harry looked from one to the other. "Do you mind if I hang out with the guys?"

And leave her and Will alone? The way things were going, that was not a good idea. Then again, if Harry wanted to be with his friends...

She shrugged and looked at Will. His jaw tightened, but he nodded. "Yeah, sure. Meet us back here in an hour."

Will watched him go, then, clearly uncomfortable, shoved his hands in his pockets and shifted from one foot to the other. "Did you meet with Judy's dressmaker?"

Another safe topic. Dena answered with relief. "Yes, and she's promised the have the dress finished by next week."

He scratched the back of his neck. "She's quick."

"She didn't have much choice."

They were like two strangers, talking in vague generalities. That stung, but at least they were talking. And Dena wanted to keep the conversation rolling. "Harry got an e-mail from Chad. If it's all right with you, he and his family are coming next month."

"Of course. It'll be good to see them."

"With all those people, you'll have a full house. We'll have to juggle bedrooms."

Now why had she mentioned *bedrooms?* These days, that was a loaded word. She thought about Will's room and sharing his bed that one wonderful, magical night. Heat pulsed through her veins. Don't go there. Swallowing, she looked up. Right into Will's eyes.

She thought she saw the awareness there, but then he blinked, and it was gone. He cleared his throat and backed up a step, as if he wanted to get away from her. That hurt.

Embarrassed and suddenly nervous, she pretended to focus on a booth across the way, where an artist was painting a flower on a small girl's cheek.

"It'll be a while before Harry gets back," Will said. "I think I'll go to the car and phone Mark about the construction schedule. With the upcoming wedding, I want to make sure he's got everything covered." He raised a brow and paused. "If you don't mind."

Mind? Pretending that she didn't love him, that his aloof behavior didn't bother her, was exhausting and giving her a giant headache. She shook her head, as eager to get away from him as he was her. "Don't worry about me. There are a couple of Little League moms over by the hot dog stand. I'll visit with them."

It wasn't fair, she thought as she headed toward her friends. While she struggled like crazy to hide her feelings, Will didn't bother to hide his. He could barely stand talking with her, couldn't wait to get away from her. Suddenly she felt awful inside, hollow and empty. Well it served her right, for falling in love with him in the first place.

For what seemed the millionth time she wished she

could call back those three little words. But she didn't regret making love with Will. She'd never regret that.

And she refused to wallow in self-pity. She pushed aside her pain and straightened her shoulders. It was time to practice what she preached, to lock her feelings away for good. Then she wouldn't have to *pretend* that she didn't love Will, because those feelings would no longer exist.

Otherwise she'd have to leave when her contract expired next month. The thought cut deep. She didn't think she could bear life without Will and Harry. But living with a man who could merely tolerate her was worse.

If she couldn't get a grip on her feelings, she would have to go.

Thunder rumbled ominously, shaking the windows. Already restless and unable to sleep, Will tossed back the covers and strode to his bedroom window. The sky was black, and a driving rain pelted the roof and glass panes in a dreary, endless rhythm.

He hoped the noise wouldn't wake Dena or Harry. Though the kid probably wouldn't hear a thing. Between an after-school Little League game and homework, he'd been beat when he fell into bed.

Will grinned, still marveling at his son's continued good spirits. Spending time together no longer meant uncomfortable silences and tension. They actually enjoyed each other. That felt damn good.

He recalled Dena's words a week and a half ago. "You've been doing a great job parenting," she'd said. While that was true, a large part of Harry's metamorphosis stemmed from her efforts. Through a labor of love, patience and persistence, she'd coaxed the boy from his dark shell.

Will shook his head in admiration. She was quite a woman. Special. He'd be smart to keep her around, offer her an open-ended contract, so she'd stay with them a long time. For Harry's sake. The kid would appreciate that.

Who wouldn't? Will remembered stopping outside his son's room last week, where he and Dena had closeted themselves. He'd spied shamelessly as she had patiently coached the boy for a spelling test.

A mother couldn't have shown more warmth and devotion.

Will knew how it felt to be the recipient of that affection. Like liquid sunshine only better. He could almost feel the soft press of her body, smell her womanly scent, taste her sweet, yielding lips. Heat uncurled in his belly.

Despite his best efforts, he wanted her. Still. More than ever. He thought about the heat darkening her eyes and the little breathless sighs she let out when he ran a thumb across her lower lip. He groaned. Given that he didn't intend to sleep with her again, that line of thinking wasn't too smart. He glanced down at his burgeoning arousal. "You hear that?"

Nope.

Rain slashed through the beam of light cast by the outdoor house lights and spattered onto the deck below. Deep in thought, Will barely noticed. Lately Dena had been subdued, but then, she'd been like that since the afternoon at the carnival. Though he'd pulled back from her in the same way, still, her behavior puzzled him. She'd all but stopped initiating conversations, and when she did talk, her sentences were short and clipped and devoid of warmth. She definitely was not in love with him, which was exactly the way he wanted things. Right? Will frowned. He couldn't shake the feeling that something was wrong.

Nothing he could pin down, but she was...distant and cool, and more tense than ever. He rubbed the back of his neck. This wasn't like her, and he was worried. He wanted things as they were before—easy and relaxed. Maybe she was just tired. Between Harry's end-of-the-school-year functions and last-minute wedding details, anyone would be.

Or maybe it was something else. Uneasy, he headed back to bed, determined to get some much-needed sleep. With any luck at all, once this wedding business was over, she'd be fine. He sure as hell hoped so.

He missed her.

"Dress rehearsals are rad," Harry said from the back of the Mercedes the afternoon before the wedding.

The kid had been chattering like a windup toy since they'd left Judy and Mark's. Just like any normal, excited eight-year-old. "Really rad," Will agreed, secreting a glance at Dena.

It was good to see her smile, and her bemused grin triggered one of his own. Despite the excitement of the upcoming wedding, she was still too quiet. She looked tired, too. Will figured he'd guessed right—she was worn out.

"Except for all that mushy stuff," Harry added.

Dena turned around and regarded the boy with raised brows. "You didn't like that jewelry box your Uncle Mark made for Judy or the love poem he glued inside it? And what about that beautiful pocket watch she gave him to hand down to their sons? I thought it was all wonderful." She let out a sigh. "Not many people are lucky enough to find the kind of love Mark and Judy share."

Red flags went up in Will's head. He threw her a sharp glance. But her gaze was fastened on Harry, and her expression innocent. Clearly she wasn't thinking about Will or her own lack of romance.

He should be relieved. So why did he have that empty feeling inside? It had been a while since lunch. Maybe he was hungry.

"Not the presents, Dena, the kissy stuff. Those guys are always kissing." In the rearview mirror Will saw his son roll his eyes. "Why do people do that?"

Though Will's attention was on the road, he felt Dena's look. So he glanced at her. Her expression was filled with unreadable emotion, which she quickly shuttered. He frowned. What was that about?

She turned her focus back to Harry. "I suppose it's a way of expressing affection," she said.

"Oh." The boy seemed to mull that over. He was silent a moment. Then he dropped his bomb. "You guys like each other. How come you never kiss?"

Uh-oh. He should have seen this coming. Harry had been dropping hints for weeks about wanting him and Dena to get together. Stifling an oath, he looked to her for help. She knew what to say in situations like this.

This time her mouth was clamped shut. And Harry

was waiting for answers. Damn. Will cleared his throat. "Dena's your nanny, son."

Though she didn't speak, her stiff posture and refusal to look at him spoke reams. His gut churned uncomfortably. He didn't like it, didn't like the tension between them, or the way that stricken look stabbed his heart. He pulled at the collar of his open-necked shirt, which suddenly seemed tight.

"But you like each other," Harry said. "I can tell. And besides, she's more than just a nanny."

A whole lot more, Will thought.

"Thank you, sweetie." She turned to smile briefly at the boy, then studied her hands. "But there are some things you're too young to understand."

Such as, kissing each other was dangerous. Will nodded. "She's right."

He glanced at his son in the rearview mirror. The small brow was furrowed. "Are you scared I won't like it if you kiss? I promise I won't mind, even if it is gross. I'll even be glad. Go ahead and do it now, and I'll prove how glad I am."

"What?" Dena's startled gaze jerked to Will's.

The whole thing would have been funny if the situation weren't so damn touchy. He stifled a grin. "We're in a car, son, and I'm driving."

"But we're almost home. You can kiss when we get there."

Will exchanged a look with Dena. For a moment her eyes warmed and darkened, beckoning him. His body responded swiftly, tightening with the familiar desire. Wise or not, he wouldn't mind tasting those lips again. Just to get the kid off their backs. "I guess we—"

"I don't think so," she interrupted, surprising him as much as Harry.

"Why not?" the boy asked.

"Yeah, why not?" Will echoed. Suddenly he wanted an answer.

"I—" Her fingers covered her mouth for a moment, and Will swore she shuddered. Then she dropped her hand and offered a wobbly smile. "You can't force two people to kiss if they don't want do. And I don't."

Will eyed her, but her face was carefully blank. He wished he knew what she was thinking.

"Would you kiss him if he wrote you a poem and made you a jewelry box?"

Dena shook her head. "It's not like that between your dad and me. We both love you dearly, but we're just…friends." Biting her lip, she turned around and stared out the window.

Thankfully, Harry didn't comment again, and they drove on in silence. A month ago she'd have chattered away, engaging both Harry and him in animated conversation as she tried to explain how things were between them.

But not now. Will rolled his shoulders to loosen the knots. He missed their lively conversations. He even missed her scoldings. Hell, he couldn't even read her facial expressions anymore.

Truth be told, he didn't much care for this new, reserved Dena. He wanted the old Dena back, the one who chided him about Harry and about working too many hours. *His* Dena. He glanced at her again. "You okay?"

"Never better," she said, but her tight smile and the rigid line of her shoulders belied the words.

Will released a heavy sigh. He'd give anything for a long, lingering look, a flush of heat on her cheeks or even a flash of anger in her eyes. He wanted to make her smile. Determined to do just that, he grinned. "There's a new comedy opening at the movie theater tonight. Anyone want to go?"

"Me!" Harry shouted.

"Dena?" Will glanced at her.

"Sorry." She shook her head. "I've got a ton to do before the wedding tomorrow. And I'm really tired. I want to get to bed early."

"Aw, heck." Harry's obvious disappointment matched Will's.

Uncertain what to do now, he shrugged. "Then I guess it's just you and me, son."

Chapter Thirteen

Dena studied her reflection in the mirror of Mark and Judy's tiny powder room. She liked the floor-length silk maid-of-honor sheath Judy's dressmaker had fashioned for her. The deep-rose color suited her well, though with those shadows under her eyes, she looked tired and a bit pale.

That was due to stress, she thought as she applied lipstick. Burying her feelings for Will and pretending that things were fine was the most difficult thing she'd ever done. Especially around Harry. She couldn't believe he'd asked her and Will to kiss, or that she'd managed to hide her surprise and longing so well. She blotted her lips absently. She was getting better at this deception business.

Too bad her heart didn't follow along with the lie. No luck there. She was still hopelessly in love with

Will. A weary sigh escaped her. And so very tired of pretending she wasn't.

And this wedding between Mark and Judy only made her feel worse. Petty. Today was their special day. She would not spoil it by moping around, wishing she had what they had. She'd pretend to be happy, just as she had the past few weeks.

Staring in the mirror, she pasted a smile on her face. It looked wooden and phony. "Come on, Dena, you can do this," she reassured, lifting her head and trying again. There, that was better. Though not quite as bright as normal. She knew she hadn't fooled Will and Harry. Both seemed to sense that something was wrong. Will hadn't questioned her about it, though she saw in his eyes that he wanted to. How could he, when an invisible wall separated them? He didn't invite her to cross it, nor did she want to. At least this way her secret—the love she carried for him—was safe, locked deep inside her, where it belonged.

But, dear God, her secret was killing her. How much longer could she hold on to it? She knew what she *should* do. When school ended and her contract expired in three weeks, she should refuse to renew it. Leave. The very thought of life without Will and Harry, of abandoning and hurting that dear, sweet boy, cut deep. Her eyes filled, and she swallowed back a sob. No. She would *not* think about this now.

She forced her freshly painted lips into a pleasant expression, then added a touch of blush. At least she had a little color now. Judy had asked her to wear her hair down. Dena ran a comb through it, then anchored a deep-pink rose behind her ear. There, she looked as festive as she ever would. She was ready for the wedding.

With a last pat to her hair she headed for the back door and yard where the ceremony would be. Through an open window, she heard Harry laugh as he and Will attached pink and purple balloons to Mark and Judy's fence.

Inexplicably the misery inside her expanded and filled her chest. She would not break down, she would not. She paused on the back stoop and pulled in a deep breath. A soft breeze tickled the air, and all along the fence balloons bumped joyously against each other. She glanced at the deep-blue sky. Not a cloud in sight. Emerald Valley weather in late May was unpredictable at best, but today the sun shone brightly, as if blessing the day. It was a great afternoon for a wedding between two people who loved each other, and she intended to enjoy it.

Hardly aware of what she was doing, she scanned the yard until she found Will. He'd taken off his tux jacket to help Harry string the rest of the balloons to the back fence. His shoulders looked impossibly broad in the crisp white shirt. Despite her aching heart, her pulse jumped at the sight of him. How she loved him.

He glanced at his son, who was intent on untangling the strings of three balloons. "Need help with those?"

Harry smiled sheepishly and held out the twisted strings. "Yeah. Too many knots."

Their relationship just kept getting stronger. They could probably get along fine without her. Dena bit her lip. Maybe it *was* time to—

"Dena, there you are." Judy's sister, Carolyn, who was going to perform the ceremony, smiled broadly. "I've been looking for you. Would you mind finishing up with these flowers while I check on Judy?" She handed Dena a fragrant basket of roses, lilacs and baby's breath.

Glad for something to take her mind off her troubles, Dena returned the smile. "Just tell me what to do."

"Thread these garlands along the ropes and the altar." Carolyn indicated the makeshift aisle that led up two steps to the grape arbor where the bride and groom planned to exchange vows.

Dena carried the flowers to the ropes and began her task. Sounds carried easily through the air. Mark calling to Harry to reassure the dogs, who were enclosed in the basement for the afternoon. The boy's excited chatter. Carolyn's laughter. Will's voice.

Somehow Dena knew that he was watching her. She looked up from her work. Even from a distance she noted the sudden warmth in his eyes. He shot her an appreciative grin. Despite her sadness she couldn't stop her responding smile any more than she could control her thudding heart. Self-conscious, she bent her head to her task. She knew without looking that he was headed her way.

He stopped beside her. "You'll get that pretty dress dirty if you're not careful."

Heat prickled her cheeks as she glanced down at the sheath. "You like it?"

"I do." He stared at her as if he'd never seen her before. Heat flared in his eyes as his gaze raked her mouth, her breasts, her hips. He still wanted her.

Her heart faltered. Unwanted warmth churned inside of her, warmth she failed to curb despite her best intentions. She loved this man, wanted him. Shamelessly. Even though he didn't return the love. She knew her feelings were reckless and dangerous, but she could no more stop them than she could stop breathing.

"You aren't going to get mad at me for saying you look beautiful, are you?"

He looked so wary that she laughed. "Of course not." It was pathetic how much pleasure his compliment brought her. "Thank you, Will."

"You're welcome." His full grin bumped up her pulse rate alarmingly. "It's good to see a smile on your face."

"That's relief, Will, because I need help while you're here." From the large basket at her feet, she handed him a rope of flowers.

They strung the garlands in silence, finishing the altar together. The heady scent of roses and lilacs perfumed the balmy air, and sunlight dappled the ground. Dena couldn't stifle her sigh. "This is a beautiful place for a wedding, isn't it?"

"Sure is," Will said, but he was looking at her.

She swallowed and adjusted a garland. "I still can't believe that in a little while Mark and Judy will stand up here and get married," she said.

"It'll be good to see my kid brother finally settled down."

"They'll be so happy together." Dena thought about the vows they would exchange and the love they shared. She was truly joyous for them. Yet, at the same time, utterly miserable for herself. Blinking back a sudden onslaught of tears, she started down the steps that led from the altar.

"Wait." Will cupped her shoulder, halting her. Concern and worry filled his eyes. "You're crying."

"No, I'm not," she lied. She forced a smile. "See?"

Clearly puzzled, he frowned. "Sure you're all right?"

No, but now was no time to discuss her troubles. "Of course," she said brightly. "I was just remembering my own wedding day. So different from this. I think I knew that day that I didn't love Reese. My parents liked him, though, and so I went ahead and married him." She shook her head. "What a mistake."

"A similar thing happened to me," Will said. "Not with the parents, but with the love thing. But Mark and Judy don't have that problem. They're wild for each other." He grinned. "They do have one problem, though." He paused to tuck her hair behind her ear, and the familiar warmth flowed through her veins.

"What's that?" she asked, sounding breathy even to her own ears.

He looked at her as if he wanted to devour her. "You could easily steal the bride's thunder. I know I won't be able to take my eyes off you." His thumb stroked her mouth.

"Careful, you're smearing my lipstick," she warned, but she couldn't stop her lips from parting or herself from wanting his kiss.

"Sorry," he murmured without a trace of regret.

And he continued to caress her lower lip. "Damn, but you're beautiful. I need to kiss you."

The warmth of his words and the heat in his eyes made her long for things she shouldn't. "We can't," she protested, even as he tugged her down the steps and pulled her behind a fat rhododendron bush.

She knew she was a fool, knew she should move away. Yet she was helpless against her desire. With a slow deliberation that left her breathless with anticipation, Will clasped her upper arms, lowered his head and dragged his mouth over hers. For one brief moment she managed to hold herself stiff and unresponsive. Then the familiar heat burned through her, obliterating her resolve and her thoughts. With a moan she wrapped her arms around his neck and melted against his rock-hard body.

She felt as if she'd come home.

Will gripped her hips, bringing her flush with his groin. He was fully aroused. "I've missed this," he growled against her lips. "I've missed you."

The dangerous confession and melting kisses unleashed her own words. "Oh, Will," she whispered between moist, fevered kisses, "if you only knew…" In the distance a balloon popped, and Harry laughed, jerking her back to her senses.

Dear heaven, what was she doing? Palms over Will's starched shirt and thudding heart, she pushed away. "No…"

"You're right." His chest rose and fell rapidly. "Not here, with a wedding about to start." Heat smoldered in his eyes as he caught her hands in his. Could he feel her trembling? "I want to make love with you again."

Her terrible longing to join with him frightened her. She could never be free of her desire for him, never be free of loving him. But he didn't want love. And she couldn't, wouldn't, give her body to him without also giving her heart and soul.

"Well, I don't." She slipped her hands free and straightened her dress.

"Can we talk about this?" Will asked.

Talk. It was what she advocated and pushed for in all relationships. Suddenly she knew what she had to do. Be honest, tell Will the truth. That she'd lied all along, that she loved him. Regardless of the consequences.

And there would be consequences. Last time she'd stated those words, he'd practically run from his bed. Until today he'd stayed away from her. That had been so very painful, and she'd ended up living a lie in order to save face. But the deception hurt even worse. Nothing could be more awful than this loneliness, this secrecy and self-imposed hell.

Her choice was painfully clear. When her contract expired in three weeks, she'd leave. She swallowed back a sob and lifted her chin. This was a wedding, a joyous time. She would not ruin it. "Yes, we'll talk. But not now. Tonight." Snatching up the empty flower basket, she spun away, toward the safety of other people.

Forty-five minutes later, with three dozen guests seated and waiting, the ceremony began. Will stood beside his solemn brother, sober-faced himself, but proud and happy as a big brother could be.

A few feet behind Mark and Judy, Harry shifted

nervously, waiting for his cue to produce the rings. Will winked reassuringly and earned a grin.

His gaze traveled to Dena, on the other side of the bride. Those sweet searing kisses had knocked him flat, but right now she looked the picture of a prim and proper maid of honor. Intent on the minister's words about love and commitment, she listened with her chin tilted and a tiny pucker of concentration between her brows.

Unfamiliar tenderness expanded his chest as he watched her. She'd probably looked the same way as a little girl in school. He would bet his new office complex that her teachers were crazy about her. It would be hard not to be.

Suddenly her eyes filled, and she bit her lip the way she did when emotion overcame her. Will tried to catch her attention, but she wouldn't look at him. Her mouth curved at the edges as if she were forcing a smile that wouldn't quite emerge.

That made him uneasy and reminded him of her cool reserve over the past few days. Which didn't jibe with the trembling, passionate woman he'd held in his arms a short while ago. Or with the turmoil in her eyes, the pain mixed with desire, that had followed in the wake of those kisses.

Foreboding filled him. Something was very wrong. Aware of the guests, he stifled a perplexed frown and pinned his eyes on the minister.

He didn't like the sorrow darkening her face. He wanted her to smile with joy or even to bawl him out. Anything, just as long as the old Dena, the head-strong, fiery woman he knew and cared for, came back. And he did care for her, deeply.

He was falling in love with her, he realized. The knowledge should have scared him spitless. Love was the last thing he wanted—or so he'd thought. Until Dena. She wasn't like his ex-wife. She was warm and loving and cared more about Harry and Will than his bank balance.

His chest filled with such warmth that he shook his head in awe. He wasn't *falling* in love, he was *in* love. Probably had been for weeks now. It had happened, and it was too late to deny the truth. Actually, it didn't feel half-bad. He grinned. Who was he kidding? It felt great.

Except for one thing. The thing that was bothering Dena. Lately it seemed that she could hardly look at him. If not for those kisses this afternoon he wondered if she had any feelings at all for him. She did— lust and then some. He'd seen that in her eyes. It was the "then some" he wanted to explore.

The minister asked Harry for the rings, and the boy proudly produced them. Everyone smiled, even Dena.

A soft breeze rustled the trees, and a bright shaft of light glinted off the blond waves of her hair, making them shimmer like spun silver. Will's mouth went dry.

Whether she was happy or sad, passionate or reserved, she was the most beautiful woman in the world. And he wanted her to belong to him alone. *His.*

Not as a nanny, but as a wife.

The thought scared him witless. But it also felt right and amazingly exhilarating.

As Mark and Judy sealed their vows with a kiss, Will made a silent vow of his own. Whatever was

bothering Dena, they'd straighten it out tonight. Together.

Then he'd ask her to marry him.

Elbows on the breakfast room table, chin propped
on her fists, and stomach knotted with dread, Dena
waited while Will tucked in Harry for the night. After
the long, festive day, the boy had headed for bed with
barely a protest.

Dena wished she could go to bed, too, bury her
head under her pillow and sleep forever. She let out
a heavy sigh. No chance of that. Tonight she had to
tell Will the truth—that she loved him. She imagined
his reaction, knowing that he'd pull away, withdraw
again. Oh, how that hurt. She hugged herself. She
would leave as soon as her contract expired.

Thanks to the generous salary Will paid, she'd
managed to save enough to attend school full-time.
She would finish her degree in two quarters and pursue her dream of counseling troubled children.

She badly wanted that dream, and just now she
latched on to it like a life raft. Yet the thought of
pursuing her goal without Will or Harry beside her
made it seem empty and meaningless. Numb and miserable, she rocked back and forth. Painful as the decision was, the time was right. Harry was strong and
healthy now. He no longer needed a full-time nanny.
With Will's love, the boy would be able to handle
her leaving well enough.

But could she? Tears filled her eyes and clogged
her throat. Perhaps she'd maintain contact for a while,
come to his games and cheer him on. She might even
continue to volunteer at his school.

But even that must end in time.

Heavy footsteps sounded on the stairs, and her heart jumped in her chest. She grabbed a napkin from the holder in the center of the table and quickly blotted her eyes. It was time to tell the truth, time to face the consequences. Feeling like a criminal about to face the death squad, she squared her shoulders.

"Harry's out cold." Will shot her a crooked grin that pumped up her pulse rate. "I've never seen him so tired. The kid was completely spent."

Despite her trepidation, Dena smiled. "He had a wonderful time today."

"It *was* a great day, don't you think?" His eyes glinted softly.

"Mark and Judy certainly enjoyed it," she said, toying with the napkin holder.

"I've never seen my kid brother so happy. That's one marriage that will stick."

Dena's eyes were on the table, yet she could feel Will's gaze. She managed a faint smile. "Anyone can see how much they love each other," she said around a tight throat.

Will looked at her oddly. "Think I'll grab a beer. Want one?"

Though Dena's mouth was dry, she couldn't swallow a thing. She shook her head. "No, thanks."

He headed for the kitchen. The refrigerator opened and shut. An everyday, ordinary sound. She bit her lip. If only she could close off her heart as easily.

Too soon he strolled back into the breakfast room. He sat down across from her. Where she could see his face. His eyes. She cringed, knowing what she'd see there when she told him the truth.

He covered her hands with his. They were big and warm and comforting. Good, strong hands, she thought. He squeezed gently.

"Whatever's bothering you, we'll work it out together."

He'd never said anything like that before. What had come over him? She gave him a long, searching look. There was a soft, tender warmth shining from his eyes that she'd never seen. It unnerved her. He'd been acting strangely since this afternoon. It had to be those kisses. Of course. He wanted her, plain and simple. Nothing more.

She was glad that he wanted her, but it wasn't enough, not without love. Sorrow filled her, for what never could be, along with a wrenching heartache unlike anything she'd ever felt. Blinking back the sudden, hot tears that had plagued her all day, she pulled her hands from his and locked them in her lap.

"Why are you crying?" he asked in a voice laced with concern.

He *would* have to act so nice. Afraid to speak or to look at him, she shook her head and stared at the table, fighting to keep her emotions in check.

"Hey." He lifted her chin with his fist, forcing her to meet his eye. His thumbs brushed away the tears, then he offered an encouraging smile. "Talk to me, honey."

He looked so earnest and attentive. That wouldn't last long. She twisted away from him and squared her shoulders. "I've done something wrong, Will, and I can't do it anymore."

"Oh?" His head tilted to the side and his eyes narrowed slightly. "Why don't you enlighten me."

Dena swallowed and rushed on before she lost her nerve. "I've been lying to you about my feelings."

"I see." In the heavy silence that hung between them, comprehension, then pain flashed across his face. Instantly his expression shuttered and hardened. "You're telling me you want to leave."

She'd hurt him. Despite her own pain, she couldn't bear that. She shook her head quickly. "No, but you might want me to when you hear what I have to say."

"So talk." He took a swig from his beer.

Dena watched his strong throat work, for some reason moved by his deep swallows. She waited for him to put the bottle down, to give her his full attention.

All too soon he did. He wiped his mouth with the back of his hand. He settled the bottle firmly on the table, gripping it in both hands as if it were an anchor.

She sucked in a breath. It was now or never. "I, um, remember when I said I talk in my sleep? I don't."

His brow furrowed. "So that speech about entertaining your friends at sleepovers—"

"A lie."

Still holding the bottle, he leaned forward, so that his face was very close. Unfortunately, his expression was unreadable. "Go on."

Dena lifted her chin and prayed for courage. "The truth is, I know exactly what I said to you that night. I love you. I know you don't want my love, and I tried to shut it off, but there are some things a person just can't control."

Afraid of what she'd see if she looked into Will's face, she stared down at her hands, still locked tightly in her lap. "I can't live like this, pretending not to feel what I feel. I need to let out my love, Will. And I need your love in return. I know that's not part of my contact, in fact, it could get me fired. But it's the truth. So now you know.'' She took her first truly deep breath in a long time and, at last, looked at him. ''The minute my contract expires, I'll pack up and be gone.''

For a disconcerting moment Will just sat there. Then he closed his eyes and squeezed the bridge of his nose between his fingers. ''Forget the contract,'' he muttered, opening his eyes. Surprisingly they were damp. ''For a few minutes, there, you had me scared.'' He gave a shaky laugh. ''I thought I'd lost you.''

''Lost me?'' Dena's mouth opened. She knew she should shut it, but it was difficult to think straight with that intense gaze zeroed in on her. He looked like a man who cared. A man in love. Hope rushed through her.

He swallowed. ''When you said you'd been lying about your feelings, I thought you were leaving Harry and me. I don't think I could handle that. Because I love you, too.''

There was something wrong with her ears. She shook her head, hard. ''Say that again.''

''I love you, Dena. I want to fall asleep with you in my arms every night and wake up beside you in the morning. I want to talk over our day at breakfast and spend my evenings and weekends with you and Harry.'' He smiled tenderly. ''Hell, I even want you to yell at me when I need it. In other words I want to be part of your life, and I want you to be part of mine. To be my wife and Harry's mother.'' He reached for her hands. "I want us to make babies together. Lots of them. Or, if you want to finish school first, that's fine, too. Just as long as we're together."

She knew she should say something, so she parroted his words. "As long as we're together. You mean that?"

He nodded soberly and squeezed her hands. "I can't promise you paradise, but I can give you my word to do everything in my power to make you happy. We belong together, Dena. What I said before, about not needing love? I was wrong, and it took me until this past week to get that through my thick skull. Will you forgive me?"

Overcome, she could only nod.

His jaw worked with emotion as his fingers tensed. "Will you marry me, Dena?"

"Oh, Will." Her eyes filled.

"Please, not again." Looking stricken, he released her hands. "Does that mean you're turning me down?"

She smiled through her tears. "Silly man, these are tears of joy. I'm happy."

He searched her face intently. "Then you'll be my wife?"

"Yes, yes, yes!"

A full grin bloomed on his face. "I'm going to buy you the biggest diamond ring in the world. Unless you'd rather have an emerald. Or maybe a ruby. Just say the word—"

She smiled tenderly. "I don't need jewels, Will. Just you."

He looked as if he'd swallowed the sun. "You've got me. Forever."

They stood at the same time, meeting around the table. Will pulled her close and sealed the vow with a tender kiss that swelled her heart.

A long while later, breathless, she smiled up at him. "Let's wake Harry and tell him the good news."

"I have a better idea. We'll tell him first thing tomorrow. Tonight I want a private celebration." His gaze heated. "Just you and me, all night long."

Dizzy with anticipation, Dena melted against him. "That sounds like the perfect plan."

Hand in hand, they headed upstairs.

Epilogue

Will spun his new wife across the dance floor, enjoying the swish of her white satin bridal gown against his tux slacks. Around the room, faces of friends and family beamed.

Harry stood proudly beside Chad and his family, who'd arrived in time for the wedding. Chad's mother, Bonnie, had gladly stood up with Dena, along with Judy, as part of the wedding party.

Next to them, Zach, his parents and several of Harry's school friends and their families were clustered together.

Dena and Will whirled past Mark and Judy and Cal and his wife and kids. Then past Will's secretary and a proud Mrs. L., and finally toward Maggie from Nannies R Us and the other nannies Dena knew.

All of them full of warmth and good wishes.

"Did you like the poem I left on your pillow this morning?" Will asked.

"Yes, and I loved the solid-gold-heart locket with pictures of Harry on one side and us on the other. You're such a romantic."

"That's easy when you're in love."

"Smile," someone shouted, and a camera flashed brightly.

"Well?" Will tugged Dena closer and tipped up her chin. "Did you smile, Mrs. Stoner?"

Radiant, she nodded. "I couldn't stop if you paid me."

"Yeah?" Will kissed her nose. "We'll see about that." Then he captured her mouth in a hot, searing kiss.

When he released her, the smile had vanished, and both of them were breathless. "I love you," he murmured.

Her eyes darkened, promising him passion and tenderness later on. "And I love you."

The music stopped, but Will held her close. In a few hours they'd board a ship bound for the Caribbean for a two-week honeymoon cruise. A long, glorious summer awaited them afterward.

In the fall, when Harry started school, Dena would, too. Will planned to continue working at the business he loved. Not as much as before. A few weeks earlier, with Cal's approval, he'd proudly instated Mark as a partner. His brother had readily adjusted to his new responsibilities and had already proved to be a valuable member of the management team.

The band struck up a spicy tune, and couples filled the dance floor. Chuckling softly, Will dipped his wife. He had everything he wanted now, a loving wife, a terrific son and a fine brother and sister-in-law. Love. *Family.*

What more could a man want?

* * * * *

Beloved author

Sherryl Woods

is back with a brand-new miniseries

THE CALAMITY JANES

**Five women. Five Dreams.
A lifetime of friendship....**

On Sale May 2001—DO YOU TAKE THIS REBEL?
Silhouette Special Edition

On Sale August 2001—COURTING THE ENEMY
Silhouette Special Edition

On Sale September 2001—TO CATCH A THIEF
Silhouette Special Edition

On Sale October 2001—THE CALAMITY JANES
Silhouette Single Title

On Sale November 2001—WRANGLING THE REDHEAD
Silhouette Special Edition

"Sherryl Woods is an author who writes with
a very special warmth, wit, charm and intelligence."
—*New York Times* bestselling author
Heather Graham Pozzessere

Available at your favorite retail outlet.

Where love comes alive™

Visit Silhouette at www.eHarlequin.com   SSETCJR

CALL THE ONES YOU LOVE OVER THE HOLIDAYS!

Save $25 off future book purchases when you buy any four Harlequin® or Silhouette® books in October, November and December 2001,

PLUS

receive a phone card good for 15 minutes of long-distance calls to anyone you want in North America!

WHAT AN INCREDIBLE DEAL!

Just fill out this form and attach 4 proofs of purchase (cash register receipts) from October, November and December 2001 books, and Harlequin Books will send you a coupon booklet worth a total savings of $25 off future purchases of Harlequin® and Silhouette® books, AND a 15-minute phone card to call the ones you love, anywhere in North America.

Please send this form, along with your cash register receipts as proofs of purchase, to:
In the USA: Harlequin Books, P.O. Box 9057, Buffalo, NY 14269-9057
In Canada: Harlequin Books, P.O. Box 622, Fort Erie, Ontario L2A 5X3
Cash register receipts must be dated no later than December 31, 2001.
Limit of 1 coupon booklet and phone card per household.
Please allow 4-6 weeks for delivery.

I accept your offer! Please send me my coupon booklet and a 15-minute phone card:

Name: _____

Address: _____ City: _____

State/Prov.: _____ Zip/Postal Code: _____

Account Number (if available): _____

---

097 KJB DAGL
PHQ4012

If you enjoyed what you just read,
then we've got an offer you can't resist!

Take 2 bestselling love stories FREE!

Plus get a FREE surprise gift!